The Orange Peel
and Other Satires

The Toby Press S.Y. Agnon Library
Jeffrey Saks, Series Editor

Books from this series

A Book That Was Lost: Thirty-Five Stories

To This Day

Shira

A Simple Story

*Two Scholars Who Were in Our Town
and Other Novellas*

Two Tales: Betrothed & Edo and Enam

A Guest for the Night

The Bridal Canopy

The Orange Peel and Other Satires

And the Crooked Shall Be Made Straight (forthcoming)

A City in Its Fullness (forthcoming)

In Mr. Lublin's Store (forthcoming)

*Forevermore & Other Stories of the
Old World and the New (forthcoming)*

Illustrated:
From Foe to Friend & Other Stories by S.Y. Agnon
A Graphic Novel by Shay Charka

THE ORANGE PEEL AND OTHER SATIRES

Including all the stories from
The Book of State

S.Y. AGNON

TRANSLATED FROM THE HEBREW

WITH ANNOTATIONS AND A FOREWORD BY
JEFFREY SAKS

The Toby Press

The Orange Peel and Other Satires
by S.Y. Agnon
With Annotations and a Foreword by Jeffrey Saks
© 2015 The Toby Press LLC

These stories, published in arrangement with Schocken Publishing House, Ltd., are available in Hebrew as part of the Collected Writings of S.Y. Agnon – *Kol Sippurav shel Shmuel Yosef Agnon*, © Schocken Publishing House, Ltd. (Jerusalem and Tel Aviv), most recent edition 1998. "Young and Old Together" appears as "*BiNe'arenu u-viZ'kenenu*" in the volume *Al Kapot haMan'ul*; the other stories in this collection appear in *Samukh veNireh*.

Unless otherwise noted, images accompanying annotations appear under Creative Commons License, CC-BY 2.0

The Toby Press LLC
POB 8531, New Milford, CT 06776–8531, USA
& POB 2455, London WIA 5WY, England
www.tobypress.com

ISBN 978-1-59264-438-4

Printed and bound in the United States

Contents

Foreword
The Metaphysics of Agnon's Political Satire
by Jeffrey Saks vii

•

YOUNG AND OLD TOGETHER
Translated by Paul Pinchas Bashan & Rhonna Weber Rogol 1

Illustrated Annotations 105

Y.L. Gordon, "With Our Young and Our Old We Shall Go" 121

•

CHAPTERS FROM THE BOOK OF STATE

Introduction
Translated by Sara Daniel 125

The Kidnappers
Translated by Isaac Franck 129

Peace Everlasting
Translated by Jules Harlow 137

The Orange Peel
Translated by Sara Daniel 147

On Taxes
Translated by Sara Daniel 153

Annotations to "The Book of State" 165

•

INTRODUCTION TO THE KADDISH
Translated by Samuel H. Dresner 169

•

About the Author, Translator & Editor 175

Foreword

The Metaphysics of Agnon's Political Satire

A COMIC MODE IS PRESENT throughout S.Y. Agnon's wide repertoire of writings. Known as a master ironist, comedic irony was a tool always at the ready, alongside other humorous tones that he could strike at will. However, when looking at his entire canon, we must recognize that, unlike his Yiddish counterpart, Sholem Aleichem, comedy was not his specialty, no matter how entertaining we find much of his writing. When examining the ethical or moral problems facing the Jewish world he wrote in the tragic genre. This is not to say that even his darkest works are without humor, and indeed, he knew well how to marshal comic relief to diffuse tension even in his most bleak depictions of Jewish history.

The stories in this collection, while not components of the backbone of Agnon's oeuvre, have significance and enduring appeal to contemporary readers for a variety of reasons. They demonstrate the artist taking his craft in a new direction – political satire. The satirist's aspiration is to amuse while arousing the reader's disapproval of societal vice by holding it up to ridicule (with a presumed didactic and remedial goal). By that measure, even these many decades after they were first published, the stories in this collection continue to both entertain and instruct. Additionally, by experiencing this corner of Agnon's corpus, we witness him in a lighter mode, and are provided with insight into some of his grandest themes, especially in regard to the shortcomings of the Jewish people and polity. By experiencing these themes being played in a minor key we reencounter them with greater appreciation in his *opera magna*.

And yet, when considering the tales in this collection on their own merits, Ariel Hirschfeld draws our attention to the artful elegance, especially of the stories of "The Book of State," through which Agnon expresses his critique of the mechanisms of society, politics, and bureaucracy, which generate important, usually adverse, effects on the State and its citizens. Gershon Shaked suggested that since social satires, by definition, are almost always more straightforwardly allegorical, leading to a more closed and unequivocal text, the genre was ill-suited to typically Agnonian story-telling which always aims for a degree of complexity supporting multiple interpretations. But who is to say how "transparent" these allegories are? Countering Shaked's critique, Hirschfeld asks: Do we truly understand what our title story's orange peel littering the public domain truly represents? Might it not be a symbol pointing in multiple directions, and isn't this a clever enough story to keep multiple ideas in play?

I would suggest that these stories are significant in an additional way, given that they offer a measure of insight into the mind of our most important modern Hebrew author. Agnon was generally reticent about exposing his personal views on matters of the day, preferring to hide between the lines of his stories or behind the mask of his narrator (who is not quite identical with the author). He once claimed that "by nature I am not a political being," and in the Introduction to "The Book of State" the narrator-author confesses his reluctance at undertaking a literary treatment of the State which is "a metaphysical concept rendered into something physical which feigns meta-physicality. When you attempt to approach it as a metaphysical entity it slips back into physicality; if one considers it in physical terms it suddenly reverts into meta-physicality."

In a posthumous record of conversations with Agnon, the author and editor David Cnaani reports him as having declared "The Book of State" to be "just a poor feuilleton [a type of light, jesting story], and I'm sorry that I even published it... I have no desire to criticize the State. We have but one small *medinah'leh*, with so many enemies, and we must protect her." I presume this is an example of Agnon being his typically playful and elusive self. Even if he understood these stories about the *medinah'leh*, that "tiny State," not to be among his greatest works, he intentionally included them when organizing them into a book collection over a decade after the first story in the cycle appeared in the newspaper. However, his comment does highlight the fact that almost all of these stories were first published prior to Israel's 1948 Declaration of Independence. The degree to which his critiques in these works still resonated by the end of his life in 1970, or still do in our present day, is a question that helps them remain compelling reading in the twenty-first century.

In this new collection of Agnon's political satires in English translation we witness the gap between the metaphysical and physical realms, between spirit and concrete, and between ideal and real – the space in which the satirist sharpens his pen like a carving knife, and reveals his opinions from behind the mask of his art. As these stories all treat themes and events in the history of early twentieth-century Zionism, they continue to fascinate contemporary readers by raising questions about the degree to which that gap remains between aspiration and implementation in Jewish life and civic society in the modern State of Israel.

In Agnon's collected works we encounter political satire in two locales. The first comes in **"Young and Old Together"** (originally published in 1920 in the Hebrew quarterly *HaTekufah*), whose title might more literally be translated as "With Our Young and With Our Old." It is Agnon's longest satire, and his first substantial literary treatment of his Galician youth. The object of the satire is something Agnon knew very well first-hand: the young Zionists of Szybusz – Agnon's literary name for his hometown Buczacz (located in today's western Ukraine) – a town whose very name telegraphs the "confusing muddle" depicted through the plot. The story's title plays off of Y.L. Gordon's Hebrew poem of the same name (which takes its biblical resonance from Exodus 10:9). As opposed to Gordon who saw mass emigration (not necessarily to Palestine *per se*) as the only viable answer to Russian pogroms of the 1880s, Agnon's "Zionist" characters organize banquets and balls. When rumors of anti-Semitic attacks in a neighboring village reach the young men of Szybusz, they board the train in a mission of support. That their initial gallantry is quickly lost amid discussions of the meals sought and eaten once they arrive is a resort to Agnon's general comedic device of depicting Jews tucking in for a meal. Gordon's poem picks up the theme of Jewish unity as a response to a pogrom, and the power of anti-Semitism to unite different strands of the Jewish people. Agnon's story plays off of this source, standing it on its head, as he paints a satirical, reverse portrait of Jewish society in Galicia. (Gordon's poem appears here following the annotations in a first-time English translation by Rhonna Weber Rogol.)

The story is set following the Austrian Parliamentary elections of 1907, and the defeat of Nathan Birnbaum (depicted in our story as Dr. Davidsohn), who stood for election as the regional representative of Buczacz and the surrounding area. Supported by the Jews and Ukrainians, his election was thwarted by alleged corruption on the part of the Poles. The story is told by a narrator, Hemdat, a young Zionist of about twenty years of age, who stands largely outside of the action he relates despite having been a witness to it. Readers of Agnon have come to recognize Hemdat, who makes cameo appearances in a variety of his stories and novels, as the author's most clearly autobiographical projection into his own writing. The annotations to this story point to some of the very many historical events and characters which populate the text, either explicitly or in thinly veiled disguises.

In the course of detailing Jewish life and society as it was, the author gives us his satirized depiction of an array of personalities, personality types, institutions, and issues of the day. Among the objects of his humor (which fluctuates from gentle mocking to acerbic biting) are the pompous windbags who pass as Zionist leaders, and the cowardice behind their words; the internecine fighting about the purposes of Zionism (whether to ameliorate Jewish suffering in Europe or to build a new Jewish settlement in Palestine); literary figures with inflated egos; the Yiddish vs. Hebrew language wars; arrogance, ignorance, and hypocrisy of rabbis, hasids, and maskilim alike; and the perennial penchant for Jews to act as their own worst enemies despite the external threats of anti-Semitism. Another target of the narrator's scorn is none other than himself: A well-intentioned youth, hungry for fame, yet seemingly incapable of any effective action. An ancillary cause for self-flagellation is the narrator's depiction of the generational divide represented by the conflict between himself and both his father and grandfather, who disapprove of his lax religious commitments and his Zionist affiliations. Hemdat's desire to gain glory as a writer, like that of his author-creator, prevents the fulfillment of his family's aspirations for him as a Torah scholar and rabbi.

The only character not to suffer the author's barbs is Alexander, a Russian Jew who escaped to Szybusz during the Russo-Japanese War. As opposed to the genteel Galician youths, depicted eating, drinking, smoking, and card-playing, Alexander is the sole character to undertake any heroic action when he fights back against a group of drunk policemen harassing a band of Jews. Thrown in prison as a result, Alexander garners neither the pity nor aid of the Szybusz Zionist youth, who see his act as unnecessarily "provoking the *goyim*."

Agnon tips his hand in the story's concluding lines: "I'm afraid they might send [Alexander] to Siberia," says Hemdat to Mr. Deixel, the pompous student leader, whose very name references his foolishness (Deixel, i.e., "*Di, ksil*," being Hebrew for: *Enough, fool!*). "Deixel rested his nose on the bouquet of flowers in his hand and inhaled the scent, after which he placed his right hand on my shoulder affectionately and said, 'Indeed, there is no complete joy in Exile.' The chains were ancient and were all rusted and were as red as blood. It appeared that the policeman was squeezing Alexander's hand so tightly that his blood was spattering onto the chains. But Mr. Deixel's flowers remained fresh and unwilted." The tragedy of Jewish history is not merely in our treatment at the hands of Gentile powers; just as often it occurs through our own self-inflictions.

Some twenty years after "Young and Old Together" Agnon took up the satirical style once again in a series of short stories published individually, but presented as chapters of a putative **"The Book of State"** (and subsequently gathered with an introduction as *"Perakim shel Sefer HaMedinah"* in his 1950 collection *Samukh veNireh*).

As is common with utopian or dystopian writers (Agnon references Bellamy at one point), who set their stories in faraway lands or times, these satires take place in some imagined future state. Literary scholar Arieh Sachs called these Agnon's Swiftian satires, portraying the Jewish society in its soon to be established State as Hebrew-speaking Lilliputians. He is correct in indicating that for Agnon and Swift, writers whose religious convictions undergird their work, pride is the sin that underlies the folly of all states and nations, as opposed to modesty as a religious virtue, and that which undermines God-given reason. Hirschfeld has drawn my attention to the likelihood that Agnon styled the collection's title as "The Book of State" with Plato's *The Republic* in mind, giving us a satirized version of the civic virtues that the great philosopher held in high regard, and the character of a just City-State and its ideal citizen.

Revisiting themes from "Young and Old Together," **"The Kidnappers"** (1942) depicts the confusion of speech-making and ego stroking with actual action or the work of alleviating societal ills. The young idealists who kidnap the blowhard public speaker are no match for his ego, and indeed their attempt to rid the body politic of the disease of windbaggery unwittingly exacerbates the problem.

Picking up on the skewering of politicians, bureaucracy, committees, etc., **"Peace Everlasting"** (1942) additionally satirizes internecine hatred, especially along religious lines. Although, like other stories in the cycle, the revealed text is largely left on the allegorical level, telling us of the tensions between and among the bared-heads and covered-heads, readers will understand the "sects" as representing the secular and religious, and might be forgiven for instantly recalling Dr. Seuss' *The Sneetches*. Both camps become the butt of the joke, but the gravity of the satire is apparent as we readers are reminded at the conclusion that while the factions were fighting amongst themselves, the foreign enemies were amassing at the border, presumably enjoying the scene as the residents of the State accomplish the aims of their own foes. A side-plot in the short story contains a satirical punch at the *Va'ad HaLashon HaIvrit* – the Hebrew Language Committee, of which Agnon was once a member, but with which he maintained a strained relationship. In fact, the year of this story's publication saw Agnon's resignation from the Committee, and the lampooning of committee work in "Peace Everlasting" no doubt has a connection to this event.

"The Orange Peel" (1939), our volume's title story, and the most well known of those in this collection, presents the narrator (who, again, we are meant to presume is a stand-in for the author himself), the self-styled "Author of the Book of State." This fellow attempts to remove a piece of refuse from the public square while others stand about debating the negligence of the State's ability to accomplish simple municipal tasks – from the most exalted officials down to the common street-sweepers. The narrator is fined for garbage removal without a license – in fact, he is the one man in the State who attempts to actively solve societal problems with his own two hands, and is rewarded by being indicted for disturbing the peace. Along the model of "for want of a nail the kingdom was lost," the small orange peel causes a chain reaction of spills, pratfalls, accidents and backups. The farce features grammarians, land-jobbers, journalists, busy-body wives of elected officials, Orthodox Jews, and a general assembly of indignant gabbers – each unhappy citizen unhappy in his own way, and each only too happy to instruct the "Author" on what should be done. In the end, the garbage remains in place, presumably to cause further nuisance, but the "Author," too, is left alone, as the policeman doesn't have time to bring him down to the station, not wanting to miss his lunch hour. Once again we have a send-up of bureaucratic inefficiencies, but also of the dehumanizing component of living life as a cog in a larger collective – a theme that occupied Agnon in a variety of ways throughout his career.

A plan to tax walking sticks and canes, the only items heretofore untaxed, in order to generate revenue and prevent a general strike among the State's workers and clerks is the subject of **"On Taxes"** (1950). The plan leads to a predictable chain of absurdities, exposing government graft and incompetence. Punchlines about the accomplishment of anything put together by a committee are too well known to even reference here. Despite being the only story in the collection to be penned after the establishment of the actual State of Israel which these tales lampoon, "On Taxes" depicts an abstract setting without specific reference to time or place. Aside from a passing mention of the idea that the State's "founding fathers were Jews" and that Hebrew is spoken there, all four of these stories might be depicting any modern state, with the "Author" presented as an Everyman. In his inability to accomplish this or that task, Agnon's narrator – his so-called dramatized ego – becomes stymied by the world he encounters. Despite our pleasure at the comic turns these stories take, the author-narrator – unlike Sholem Aleichem's *schlemiels* – has to manage devoid of humor, slapstick or otherwise, because these tales capture something of the high anxiety generated by the encounter with modernity in all its guises. As opposed to "Young and Old Together," where Deixel and Co. are pompous buffoons, and undermine the Zionist cause they claim to promote, in "The Book of State" the very institutionalizing of these archetypes into the machinery of bureaucracy – itself a partial fulfillment of Zionism's aspirations – gives rise to malice and evil. Instead of being pointed at the individual speech-makers and paper-pushers, these satires reach razor sharpness when targeting the collective.

Prof. E.E. Urbach noted internal connections and motifs in these stories, as well as in the surrealistic, modernistic tales in "The Book of Deeds" (*Sefer HaMa'asim*), also contained in *Samukh veNireh*. They all examine the actions of individuals in the framework of larger society, as depicted nightmarishly in "The Book of Deeds" when the narrator, wishing to perform some seemingly mundane task – mail a letter, catch a bus, reach his home, celebrate a holiday, etc. – becomes entrenched in complications put forth by some larger force, leading him to helplessness and deviance from his path. As journalist Ari Shavit recently observed, "As the State became everything, the individual was marginalized." "The Book of State" stories, while not "Kafkaesque" in the same way (a comparison Agnon bridled at), humorously show how a private citizen attempts to save the State from its troubles and enemies, while the State turns its citizens into fools and knaves, depriving them of their liberty. Whether deterred by heaven above (in *Sefer HaMa'asim*) or a committee chamber below (in *Sefer HaMedinah*) the narrator never stands a chance.

The first two sections of this anthology touch on certain common themes and strike similar notes in ways that should be obvious to the reader. Please note that these two works, "Young and Old Together" and the collection that makes up "The Book of State," do not appear in the same volume of Agnon's Hebrew writings. Nevertheless, despite their similarities as political satires, when placed side by side the element that separates them should become distinctly pronounced. While they both explore issues of Jewish use of power and the effects of powerlessness, alongside skewering Jews as agents of that power, as well as depicting those on whom the agents act, they do so from opposite vectors. "Young and Old Together," set in the *alte heim* in 1907, portrays the effects of *insufficient* Jewish power, a few short decades before the catastrophic events that neither the characters nor Agnon (writing in 1920) could have possibly imagined. "The Book of State" stands on the other side of the historic breach, foreseeing Jewish sovereignty in a Jewish State, yet understanding that it would be neither a messianic nor a utopian era. There would still be objects to satirize, and that in and of itself is reason enough to mourn – the subject of our anthology's third section, **"Introduction to the Kaddish"** (1947).

While he could allow himself to be satirical in regard to the Zionist enterprise, or the State during its founding, at a certain point his thinking took a decidedly un-comedic turn. Agnon appended his "Introduction to the Kaddish" as a coda to "The Book of State" stories when they were collected in book form. While we have no indication from him why he did this, we know that the organization of material within each collection was done deliberately, and we can speculate that the placement of this profoundly serious, short, liturgical piece was motivated by both religious and Zionist fidelities. To read any element of satire or cynicism into it (as some mistakenly have) is a disservice to the work and its author.

Following a medieval tradition of a poetic "*petiḥah*" (opening) to a prayer, in which the themes of the piece of worship to be introduced are highlighted or expanded, Agnon prepared this introduction to the Mourner's Kaddish in 1947 to be recited "for the fallen defenders of the Land of Israel." James A. Diamond trenchantly points out that the expansion of the well-known Kaddish was necessary in 1947, as the tally of the Six Million was still being undertaken, and the human sacrifices in defense of the fledgling Jewish homeland were growing day by day. It is composed against the question of what it means to salvage the religious metaphors of serving and standing guard at the palace of a King who may have appeared to have abandoned His troops. But even in this most serious of works, the themes of "The Book of State" are reflected, albeit in a wholly somber tone: the sanctity and supremacy of each individual, even when he is marshaled as part of an army arrayed in defense of the collective body politic.

> *Each one of us is as important in His eyes as a whole regiment.*
> *For He does not have many to set in our place.*
> *Thus if one Jew dies (God forbid),*
> *Distress falls upon the regiments of the King,*
> *And a weakening comes to the kingdom of He who is Blessed,*
> *For His kingdom lacks one of its regiments*
> *And the greatness of He who is Blessed is lessened.*

The death of each individual causes a lessening of God's kingdom on earth, therefore we recite the Kaddish, imploring *Yitgadal ve-yitkadash shemah raba* – praying that His name should be magnified on high to rectify His own diminution caused by the loss of each member of the collective below. As opposed to treatments of this theme in his works of fiction, this is Agnon's attempt to compose liturgy (indeed, it is still ceremoniously recited at Memorial Day events throughout Israel). Unlike so much of his writing, he does not here create a pastiche of holy source material in an ironic subversion of those pious texts. Writing in Jerusalem in 1947, as the ashes in

Europe were first settling, and the conflagration in *Eretz Yisrael* was just beginning, he set satire aside.

✎ ✎ ✎

Acknowledgements

"The Kidnappers," translated by Isaac Franck appeared first in *Jewish Frontier* 39:4 (May 1972), pp. 9-12. "Peace Everlasting," translated by Jules Harlow, appeared first in *Conservative Judaism* 19:2 (Winter 1965), pp. 32-39. "Introduction to the Kaddish," translated by Samuel H. Dresner, appeared first in *Conservative Judaism* 11:2 (Winter 1957), pp. 2-4. These three stories are republished here in revised and modified form. All other translations, and all annotations of the stories, are original to this volume.

The opportunity to collaborate with translators Sara Daniel and the duo of Paul Pinchas Bashan and Rhonna Weber Rogol was as pleasant as it was enriching, and provided me with fresh insights into these stories. Rabbi Jules Harlow very graciously participated in reexamining and revising his translation of "Peace Everlasting," now a half-century after its initial publication.

I am grateful to the following scholars of Hebrew literature, fellow Agnonists all, for their encouragement and assistance in the research for this volume: Omer Bartov, Haim Be'er, Hillel Halkin, Avraham and Toby Holtz, Rachel Manekin, Elchanan Reiner, Avi Shmidman, Rafi Weiser, and Hillel Weiss. Ariel Hirschfeld and Alan Mintz have been especially helpful as friends, teachers, and guides.

Jeffrey Saks
Editor, The S.Y. Agnon Library
The Toby Press

Young and Old Together

Assembly of voters in Buczacz, 1907. The Zionist candidate Nathan Birnbaum is at bottom center (holding folded overcoat on right arm). The young S.Y. Agnon (né Shmuel Yosef Czaczkes) appears toward bottom right of the photo, with mustache, arms folded, head tilted to his right.

Chapter One

We Escort Dr. David Davidsohn as He Leaves Town

The train stood at the railway station, passengers peeking out of the windows, and two or three people hastened hurriedly by and were engulfed by the steam of the engine. The start of the journey had been slightly delayed and we stayed around to bestow honor upon our candidate, Dr. David Davidsohn, at the hour of his departure. Our candidate, Dr. David Davidsohn, who had not been elected, was returning to his hometown and we, the young Zionists of Szybusz, had come to pay our last respects. How we loved him and his speechmaking. How we adored his countenance and his discourses. He could even converse in Yiddish and even attended synagogue on the Sabbath before the elections. A pox upon those who claimed that he had done so deceitfully, just to capture the hearts of the people so that they would vote for him, for he had lived in Vienna for several years and had never gone to pray. It never occurred to them that he had gone out of love, out of love for the people who had chosen him to be their representative. There are many doctors in the world who write books of praise for the Torah and its commandments, even though they don't fulfill all of the commandments that are in the Torah. Deeds are not the essence, but rather the radiance of Judaism.

Not only had the Zionists come to escort Dr. Davidsohn, but some simple Jews also had come; however those had returned home in the middle of the procession. But we, the young Zionists, didn't budge from his side even when he had boarded the train. To tell the truth, there were two or three among us who had wanted to head back right away but because they had shared a carriage ride with us, they also stood and waited.

It had been a day in early summer. The cherry trees were blossoming strawberries were sprouting from the earth, the winter clothes had already been stored away in the closet, and the air of the world was clear and pleasant, warming the cockles of one's heart. The scent of the tar seeping from the railroad ties, which blended with the aroma of the fresh grasses, aroused in one's soul wondrous yearnings for faraway places. Vienna, Dr. Davidsohn's hometown to which he was returning, loomed large on the horizon. Oh, how distant she was, and yet so close to our hearts! His intoxicating eloquence had not yet faded. Orations that were given in those great days would inspire the heart. Each time a word or a phrase would be mentioned, we would be extremely moved. Even the mediocre ones among us, who never had dared speak up against those more forceful and would bow their heads in the face of each and every decree, now hurled words of insolence even against the authorities. They recognized that they had been misguided and were not slaves to the authorities, but rather that the authorities exist to do their will, which is the will of the people.

Even though our candidate had not been elected his downfall was not a failure, for his defeat was not for lack of votes but rather caused by our opponents' misdeeds, the likes of which had never before been seen anywhere in the world. Here, we will relay just one of many stories. When one voter arrived to cast his vote and the Bürgermeister saw that he intended to vote for Dr. Davidsohn he said, "This man is on the dole," and the voter was disqualified. You may be inclined to assume he was a pauper, but he was actually a wealthy moneylender. Yet his clothes were shabby, in the manner of the people of Szybusz who do not dress extravagantly. For had they done so it could have led to the desecration of God's Name, because the Gentiles would indict the Jews, saying, "You have a lot of gall, living off public funds and then daring to show off." And not only that, but several fraudulent ballots were cast in favor of the opposing candidate. Even the dead were casting ballots in that candidate's name. One Itzhak Mundschpiel was even found wandering around the polling station announcing, "I have come to greet my ancestors, may they rest in peace, who have come from the world beyond." And we fervently fantasized that when the legislative session would convene and all the delegates had gathered, Adolph Stand, head of the Zionist Club, would immediately stand up and proclaim, "In this way so-and-so got elected to the legislative body." At which very moment, the big shots would become appalled and jump up proclaiming, "We can't reside under the same roof with that one." And right away the chief officer would appoint a special committee of men of truth who hate unjust gain to call for new elections in Szybusz, and the people would come to vote in Dr. Davidsohn, bring him immediately to the legislative hall and erect for him a podium of honor from which he would orate and be a luminary for the people, all of whom would walk in his light.

Chapter Two

When the Pogroms Erupt

While we were standing at the train station, we heard a rumor that the Jews of Pishevits were being beaten. I'd already heard this rumor in the morning at the study house, but I didn't give it its full due because at that moment I had been in the middle of the morning prayers and didn't want to stop, lest it be said that Zionists are not vigilant when it comes to prayer.

Pishevits is a small town near our city. Pishevits's shopkeepers obtain their merchandise from Szybusz, the daughters of Pishevits's poor work as servants in Jewish homes in Szybusz, and the craftsmen of Szybusz gaze upon their beauty and take wives from amongst them. In Pishevits there is a tobacco factory that employs many workers, who are Christian Socialists well known for their hatred of Jews.

Sigmund Deixel stood up declared, "All those who still nurture even a spark of nationalism within their hearts, should rise and go to Pishevits to rescue their brethren from the pogrom!" He hadn't even finished speaking when several young men who had been standing with one foot inside the train and the other outside of it, pulled their other leg inside the train so that they could go to Pishevits and defend their brethren there. They said, "It's not words that are of the essence, but action. It's no great feat of bravery to make heroic speeches while standing idly by at a time when they are plotting to destroy us. What will the people of Pishevits do, living as they do in a town that is mostly Gentile, and how will they stand up to their enemies without help from the outside? As if it's not enough that they have been deprived of their rights and that their candidate has been disqualified, now they are trying to take away their very lives."

Mr. Deixel went on and added, "If I go, you surely must go. If I am going to Pishevits, although obliged in my representative capacity as president of the Student Zionist Association to attend Mrs. Zilberman's speech today, then all the more so you must go to Pishevits." His words made an impression on his listeners and even the weak ones amongst us were filled with courage and boarded the train.

Almost all of us came from good families. We spent our days working on the Zionist cause. On the eve of the Day of Atonement we would stand before the collection plates in the synagogues and study houses, collecting small change for benefit of the Jewish National Fund. On Hanukkah, we would throw a Maccabee Ball and on winter nights we'd visit our female friends who belonged to the "Ruth Sisterhood" and who gave biweekly lectures about the history of Israel. Since they didn't understand German, we would read to them from the abridged edition of Graetz and translate the words for them, and from that they would prepare lectures in Polish. At times, we would buy oranges from the Land of Israel and sell them at a profit for the benefit of the national fund. The rest of the escort party, some of whom were small time merchants and some of whom were artisans, had campaigned with us in the elections. Since they had spent time in the company of Dr. Davidsohn, some of his glory had rubbed off on them. As the Talmud says, "The Duke took hold of me and the scent of royalty was absorbed into my hand." And when they heard that a pogrom had befallen Pishevits they said, "Relief and deliverance will come to the rich from the government, which protects them. But who bears the brunt of every trouble? The poor do. And if we don't come to their rescue, then who will save them?" They hastily climbed the stairs of the railway car and rode with us to Pishevits.

And here it is fitting to mention one young Jew who was with us on that trip. In truth, he has already been included in the other group, the artisans, and so on, but since I'm going to expand upon his story in upcoming chapters I'll just give a small preview, so it won't appear that he suddenly jumped into the picture. This young man was named Alexander and in the days of the Russo-Japanese War he had somehow wound up in Szybusz, worked as a blacksmith's apprentice and become engaged to a housemaid from Pishevits. He was short in stature and his face looked like a Russian Gentile, so that were it not for the Jewish obstinacy that burst forth from between his eyes, you would never have known he was a Jew. He would lend me books from the Bund and I loaned him Mendele's *The Mare* which he has yet to return to me. Why would Alexander, a member of the Bund, have chosen to escort Dr. Davidsohn? Only because the day in question was the second festival day in the Diaspora and his shop was closed, and he was going to meet Peshi Shaindel his fiancée from Pishevits. As it says in the Talmud, "A man's feet are responsible for him; they take him to the place where he is wanted."

Peshi Shaindel was a maid, the daughter of Pesach the Teacher, and she served in Dr. Zilberman's house. She had another quality which was that she was literate, and she was involved with the Socialists and even the students among them did not refrain from conversing with her. Who among us is greater than Deixel, who was a Social Democrat, and he used to go with her hand in hand. And even after he eschewed Socialism and became an adherent of Zionism, he still went with her hand in hand. And she still would come to him to borrow books. There is no doubt that she enjoyed the company of that student, because from him she was fortunate enough to learn some new ideas of which no one in her family had been aware. In any event, in my opinion there was a fly in that ointment, because Peshi Shaindel began comparing Alexander to Deixel. And once, when Alexander took her hand in his she remarked, "How beautiful Deixel's hands are." "Deixel," she said, and not "Mr. Deixel."

Sitting comfortably on soft, red velvet seats on the train, in second class next to the doctor, alleviated our worries about the pogrom. The joy of youth was rekindled and new, good feelings filled our hearts. We were happy to leave our town for a little while and go on a trip, and all the more so as we were sitting the whole way with Dr. Davidsohn, and all the more so as we were on our way to save a Jewish town.

One of the group members piped up and said, "Do you know what, let's sing "*HaTikvah*." Let our foes both hear and see that we don't fear them."

Deixel got up and extended his right arm like the conductor of an orchestra. We rose immediately to our feet and began to sing the lyric, "Our hope is not yet lost."

The doctor looked at him affectionately and a slight smile graced his lips. That Deixel really knows how to sing a verse in a song. We hadn't even reached the second stanza when our throats froze wordlessly. Wonder of wonders, all these years we had been singing the anthem "*HaTikvah*" and we'd never realized that we didn't know anything but the beginning. Seeking inspiration we started singing in Polish and German, songs such as "There by the Cedars" and "Hear, O' Brothers," Zionist songs that were going around the country. And thus we sang until the singers got tripped up on a song and returned to discussing the pogrom.

One of the members of the group said, "It's a pity. I have a sturdy cane at home and I didn't bring it along." This is like the adage told in Szybusz that goes, "The hand is ready to shake the Lulav frond, but the beadle has locked the citron in his house." Vovi Mundschpiel said, "It would be worthwhile for the press to note about this trip that for once the Jews traveled without luggage."

The conductor came in to check the tickets. One of our group got up and slipped him some change and thus we were able to use our third class tickets without paying second class fares. Dr. Davidsohn was taken aback and finally gave a smile, perhaps out of anger or perhaps out of shock.

This was the nicest trip I had ever taken. The doctor recounted events that had occurred in earlier days, such as when he and his students would take trips out of town and, not being used to seeing Jews dressed in Christian garb, the young Gentiles would stand bewildered not knowing whether they should throw rocks at them like they did at all the other Jews. It didn't take long before they realized the truth and their hands, the hands of Esau, did what they always do. The doctor's story gladdened our hearts. All Jews are brethren. Even a Jew in Christian garb is still a Jew. Alexander stood in a corner and said nothing. I put my hand on his shoulder and told him, "I see you are not much interested in our discussion, in which case sing us some Russian songs as we've depleted our repertoire and I'm sure our friends would love to hear a new song." Alexander jumped up from his place as if stricken by a rock from a catapult. Finally he answered me with a snarl and kept silent. The fact that he was going to Pishevits troubled him greatly. There was nothing new for him about pogroms. It was by way of a pogrom that he had become orphaned from his father and his mother. And when the pogroms became widespread, he had joined up with the defense organizations until the outbreak of the Russo-Japanese War when he escaped to Galicia. It was not out of fear that he had run away, but out of principle so as not to be killed for the benefit of Reactionary Russia. The conductor blew his whistle and announced, "Pishevits!"

Chapter Three

A Division of the Hearts

The train arrived in Pishevits and we had arrived at the purpose of our trip. We parted from the doctor and alighted from the train car. The parting was hard on us and we stood like mourners at the train station and waved our handkerchiefs at the dear doctor standing at the window. His short beard with its silver streaks glistened with Jewish charm. The train began to move and rolled on until it disappeared into the distance. Dust, soot and sweat covered our tired faces, but our eyes shone as if emerging from a morning dream. We stood briefly at the train station and wiped the sweat off our faces with the handkerchiefs that we had been waving at the doctor. Suddenly we realized that there was nothing for us to be doing at the station and we set off. There were those amongst us who said we should divide up into small parties as there was nothing to fear and because one cannot abandon the entire town and save only one street. But there were those who said on the contrary, that so long as we remained as one pack we would be able to instill fear and if we tried to rescue the whole city we would risk losing everything by attempting too much. Who are we and what power have we to decide that one street's blood is redder than the next, rather we should set up a watch there since defense consists of nothing but "sit still and do not act." In other words, we are not coming to defend the town by deed but rather by our very appearance in the town. Therefore, it is ill advised to split up into small teams, because as long as we stick together as one group everyone will be intimidated by us. Although our opinions differed from each other, those in favor of splitting up did not refuse to go along with their opponents, so that they could show them later that they'd been wrong. Thus we arrived in town united as one.

Chapter Four

The Camp That Is Left Behind

The town was quiet, the shops were open and the shopkeepers stood in the entranceways, tugging at the cloaks of passersby. Some of the houses had broken windows, but you could tell from the paper that was patching over the cracks that the destruction was not new. And that ambience of springtime that is felt in the smallest of towns imparted a holiday-like mood upon the peaceful streets.

Someone from the group said, "First things first, let's eat lunch."

His words were very timely, as we were already standing at a crossroads, not knowing which way to go. And we still hadn't decided which inn to visit until Vovi Mundschpiel came and said, "Let's go to the inn of The Infamous Maidservant." Everybody heard and asked incredulously, "Where?!" Vovi responded, "I said, 'The Infamous Maidservant.'" Veixel asked in shock, "In the middle of the day!?" Said Vovi to Veixel, "You pig! Your question betrays your thoughts. The Infamous Maidservant is the name of a legitimate establishment."

One of the group stood up and said, "Make haste friends, lest the food get cold." We got up and went, and as we walked we sang, "Bear Your Banner to Zion, the Banner of the Tribe of Judah." At this point the down-and-out who couldn't afford to eat at the inn went to the homes of their relatives and we went in to eat. There were those who ate a complete meal and those who just had a bite. When we heard that there were dumplings we jumped for joy, for the dumplings of Pishevits had a great reputation in Szybusz. When we had eaten our fill we ordered more of those dumplings for dinner. Deixel got up and went to the bar and drank half a pint of liquor and took out a cigarette to smoke. Saltzman drank fruit juice, while Mundschpiel chatted with the barmaid. Some of our group joined him. Even though she was not really attractive, we were jealous of our friends who were worldly enough to strike up a conversation with a girl, like a man speaking with his friend. Finally, we got up and went out to the marketplace.

Chapter Five

Through the Streets and Through the Squares

The streets of the town were enveloped at that moment with the tranquility of summer afternoons. A multicolored assemblage of pigeons sat on the rooftop corner warming themselves in the sun, a large and fat pig rooted in the garbage and a colt neighed in the distance. Some of the shopkeepers sat by the doors of their shops and others sucked on thin cigarettes and conversed with their neighbors. In the morning when they had been expecting customers they hadn't noticed us, but now that the customers had left the market they began to interact, heaping upon us an abundance of flattery. Those who acquired merchandise from our fathers in Szybusz began extolling our fathers' wealth and homing in on us. Even their wives greeted us warmly and with every word they beamed at us like women of valor. The young women of the town stood at the windows and peeked at us with a mixture of curiosity and bashfulness. When we glanced back at them they looked away. Finally, we got up and went on our way. Everyone with a stick in his hand was walking tapping on the stones, on the briar and the brambles. In this way we progressed through the town until we arrived at the Hill of the Slaughtered, that being the Hill of the Slaughtered which is the burial place of two hundred

Jews who had been martyred when Chmielnicki had assaulted the town and the Poles had handed them over, after falsely swearing to protect the Jews with their own lives. Here in this place a brilliant idea popped into our heads, namely that if pogroms were to break out in the city we would draw the enemy here. For here on this hill the Jews of Pishevits would awaken and remember that they have no one to rely on but themselves and would no longer proffer their necks to their oppressors.

Chapter Six
And It Is Said About the Nations

That evening Mr. Levi Cohen invited us for supper. Mr. Levi Cohen was the head of the Zionists in Pishevits. Despite being a moneychanger and a rich man, he was a loyal Zionist. He subscribed to two Zionist newspapers, to the Yiddish daily *Tagblatt*, and to the Polish *Voskhod*. In order to remind himself of his childhood learning, two and half years ago he borrowed from me two issues of *HaShachar* and loaned me a book by the humorist Sapir, and the poem, "The Shepherd Among the Lilies," which had been translated by another resident of the town, Mr. Miefurst, from French to German.

The dining room was brightly lit, the table was set, the walls were decorated with paper flowers, and a cluster of waxen grapes added beauty to the table. The portraits of Herzl, Max Nordau and Rabbi Shmuel Mohilever were nicer than mine, for mine were small and I had cut them out of Gershom Bader's yearbook, while his were large and hung in gilded frames. Mrs. Matilda, his wife, a petite and agile lady, the sister of my friend Hofmann, showed off her cooking and baking skills. Each and every dish was excellent in both taste and appearance. Mrs. Matilda said, "Even though I live in a small town, nonetheless I have no reason to be ashamed of my cooking, even by Szybusz standards. Let these pampered ones who left their homes without a meal eat and enjoy." She had prepared dairy dishes as is fitting for suppertime during the summer months. The host said to Deixel, "Mr. Deixel, do you know why my wife prepared a dairy meal a not a meat meal? So that a certain pious man would not have to deprive himself of eating meat in an unfamiliar place." This was a double joke because after all Deixel wasn't particularly careful about eating only kosher meat, plus the house of Mr. Levi Cohen was an observant one. Deixel replied and said, "Mr. Cohen, a joke for a joke. Why did the Almighty slaughter the leviathan and salt it to keep for the righteous ones in the world to come but leave the wild bull to graze in the desert?" And in the middle of his words, Mr. Deixel paused and took a leisurely drink of water so as to give his listeners a chance to consider the question and said in a drawn out fashion, "So that the righteous ones could eat the fish, and not have to deprive themselves of partaking from His slaughter." Everyone sitting around the table smiled, laughed and chuckled except for me, as I was annoyed at Deixel for having told the joke without giving proper attribution. When Deixel adorned his speeches with sayings of the sages and adages of the righteous that he had heard from me, I never complained to him, as we don't question the methods of those working for the national good. But in this case, what would it have hurt him to mention my name? Mundschpiel said, "Until such time as we are privileged to eat from the leviathan, let's eat these appetizing sardines that Mrs. Matilda has placed in front of us." Said Yaakov Shimshon, the son of the ritual slaughterer, "I read in Sokolow's newspaper *HaTzfirah* that sardines are the dish of small, fried fish mentioned in the Talmud. The host said, "Sokolow goes under the pen name of Ahad Ha'am." "Not so," I said and reddened, "Rather Ahad Ha'am and Sokolow..." I hadn't even had a chance to finish pointing out the host's error when they began bringing out, one after the other, potato soup, bread crusts fried in butter, cheese blintzes with raisins and plum cake.

After the meal Mr. Cohen asked the guests, "Do you gentlemen smoke?" And he instructed that the cigarette box be brought in. Even I took a cigarette, but the pleasure was incomplete as I was disappointed that the cigarette package didn't come from the Zionist factory in Cracow, which puts a Star of David on its packaging.

The host sat Mr. Deixel on the plush chair by the window and sat opposite him and regaled us with stories from the time of Bloch and Bick. There have never been such good days for the Jews as those days, for in those days the weak were made strong. There was a story about a tailor who chased a provincial official with his cane and called out, "You scoundrel, you forged the voters' roll!" And another story about a certain Hasid who grabbed a woman in the marketplace, and danced with her out of joy that Bloch had been elected. The upshot was that every election has paled in comparison with the first ones. After Bloch and Bick, a Christian ran against a Jew. Those elections were meaningless. The priest passed his flock under the cross and made them swear that they would not vote for anyone but their Christian brother and the Jews voted for the Jew. It was almost as if the whole affair was not worth dealing with. After those elections, a Jew vied once again with a Jew. And even those elections were inconsequential. There was a story of certain rich and distinguished physician from Russia whose wife ran away with her lover to Vienna and he wanted to make her jealous so he decided to get himself elected to the Austrian legislature (apparently the fool wasn't aware of the adage of one of our Rabbinic sages that a woman will suffer frugal living if accompanied by romance) And should you wonder, "Is he not from Russia and what would a Russian subject have to do with the Austrian legislature?," as it is said, "money solves everything." He went to see your Bürgermeister Zanvil and bribed him with a great deal of money and Zanvil gave him citizenship rights in Szybusz. And not only did he bribe Zanvil, but all the clerks and all those involved in public service profited from him. Nonetheless, they voted for his opponent with the exception of a few fools who assumed that because they had taken his money they were obliged to sell him their souls. After the physician had squandered his own fortune and that of his family on that affair, he died of shame and his opponent was elected, to the glory of the Jews.

How great was that era, and we have not witnessed even its pale reflection. Woe to us for being born into a generation as bereft as ours.

The hostess brought out a photograph album to show us a picture of Bloch wrapped in a prayer shawl like a rabbi. While she was searching she found a postcard with the portrait of an impressive looking gentleman on it. One of the guests asked, "Who is this?" Cornelia, the hostess's young daughter looked and said, "A thick-bearded Jew." The hostess looked at her daughter scornfully and said, pausing after each word, "Gamliel Pedhazur ben Shaltiel Isaac Tintenfass." "Gamliel Pedhazur ben Shaltiel Isaac Tintenfass," I repeated in one breath. "Tintenfass!" cried my friends in amazement. "That's Tintenfass and that's his signature. Tintenfass and his handwriting. His very handwriting and in blue ink." The hostess said, "I hadn't realized that he was so renowned. My brother-in-law the student sent it to me from Lemberg. Cornelia, don't touch it so you don't get it dirty." And as she said it, Mrs. Cohen was already wiping off the postcard.

Everyone who knows me knows that I don't seek grandeur for myself but at that moment I wished to be famous. Had I been famous I would have composed a nice verse for our hostess in gratitude for her having worked so hard for us. Not like Tintenfass and all the other prominent ones, who assume that ink exists only for authors to sign their names with. At the same time that I was wishing for greatness for myself, it dawned on me that I am just like all the others, and that it was only because I was one of the group that had come from Szybusz that Mr. Cohen had invited me over, and if there had been someone else in my place he would have been invited; it wasn't because I am me that he invited me, rather because I was one of the group. And this realization both saddened and affronted me. Deixel pointed to the photo of Tintenfass and said, "There's a man for you, a Jew and a European rolled into one. I could actually call him a modern man, neither idle nor obstinate. He solved the Hebrew and Yiddish problem." How? Mr. Deixel immediately quoted in Polish from one of the articles of our illustrious author that had been published in a Polish-Zionist periodical. Deixel said, "Tintenfass said 'I speak Yiddish yet truly I meditate on Hebrew day and night.'" And in this manner Deixel went on, quoting the entire article by heart. Things that had been deliberated about for many years, our brilliant author delivered to us at the tip of his quill. Mr. Deixel went on and said, "When I was in Lemberg, my friends Doctor Shebishifleinu and Doctor Sternhimmel and Doctor Himmelstern and Professor Tzigenmilch and Leopold Nachtmahl" (clearly he knew the latter very well which is why he didn't preface his name with Mister) "told me as follows: 'We're surprised at you, our friend, for not inviting Tintenfass to Szybusz and for not throwing a Tintenfass Ball in honor of Tintenfass'." The host commented, "It's no wonder that they say you men of Szybusz are gluttons. We here don't have the wherewithal to put together even an ordinary ball while those Szybuszites have to have a Tintenfass Ball?!" Deixel exclaimed, "A ball!" At that moment the host's eyes filled with joy. The host had found in Deixel's word a glimmer of hope that a ball would materialize.

Chapter Seven
A Silver Lining

Said Deixel, "Every cloud has a silver lining. We came because of pogroms and in the end we'll bring about a ball. I'll tell you the truth, if you don't act quickly, the Social Democrats will. I'll tell you more generally, it's not that hard to make a ball." Mr. Cohen asked bewildered, "Making a ball is not that hard? How so?" Mr. Deixel answered, "It's simple, isn't it? The president goes up to the podium and gives the opening remarks, not really a speech just two or three words by way of benediction, not less than ten minutes and no more than a quarter of an hour. For the main speech, namely the keynote address, you need to get someone from out of town. If you like I'm ready to ask my friends, either Gold the student or the apothecary Zilber to come and deliver the keynote. The truth is that even if they promise, they won't show up. But…" Deixel hadn't yet a chance to finish when Mr. Cohen cut into the middle of his remarks and said, "Many times we've tried to organize a ball, but we weren't successful. It's beneath someone who's a doctor to give a speech in a small town. Really, we would have settled for a speaker who was not a doctor, after all we're not particularly spoiled, but even the students aren't eager to come here because there is no Polish correspondent here to report in the *Voskhod* that a certain student lectured here. And as such we are in trouble for the folks don't know the meaning of nationalism, and if they were to found a branch of the Goldmann Circle, assimilators with a widespread presence all over the country, ultimately even our followers would leave us and go to a Goldmann Circle, initially to read free newspapers and in the end to become assimilated." "But…" said Mr. Deixel, "between us I'll tell you that you won't lose out at all if Gold and Zilber don't come and speak. With them it's always the same speech and the same thing. And you get sick get of hearing it. During Hanukkah what do they say? Once we had Maccabees and now we have Zionists. During Passover what do they say? In Egypt we had Moses and Aaron and now we have Herzl and Nordau. For whatever trouble befalls us, the same words and the same old speech." The host smiled and said, "If so, we don't let just anybody speak." Mr. Deixel replied, "Idolize Gold, idolize Zilber, but above all idolize the truth." Suddenly Deixel rose to his full height and said, "For the sake of Zionism I shall not keep silent and for the sake of our ideals I will not remain quiet until the ball is organized and I myself will give the speech. Even though I already have had my fill of speechmaking, all the more so now when I'm facing my final exams." Mr. Cohen and then Mr. Notkiss, secretary of the Pishevits Zionist Association, shook hands with Deixel affectionately.

Mr. Deixel continued and said, "The ball is as good as arranged, and even those who are not Utopians like Bellamy and so on can already hear the sound of clapping from all of Pishevits, although we still need to look into the matter of the recitation. Any young girl can do a recitation in Polish, but who's going to do a Hebrew recitation?"

The lady of the house served Mr. Deixel a piece of Suchard brand chocolate. "A piece of chocolate, gentlemen?" she said to the rest of the guests. "Suchard chocolate!" announced Deixel like a connoisseur as he leisurely broke off a small piece and put it into his mouth.

Mr. Cohen repeated, "And so what are we going to do about the Hebrew recitation?" Relishing the chocolate cake, Deixel said, "And where is Cornelia?" Said Mr. Cohen, "What does Cornelia have to do with a Hebrew recitation?" Still savoring the chocolate Deixel said, "My feeling is that you won't find anything more appealing than

Cornelia wrapped in white with a blue sash around her waist and a Star of David in her hair, as she ascends the stage and reads a Hebrew poem." All the gathered ones responded, "Hooray!"

The lady of the house said, "Thank God there is no shortage of white dresses, and as far as a blue sash is concerned I'm sure we can find one." Little Cornelia blanched in fear. Even though she had no idea what a recitation was, her heart told her that no good could come of this for her.

Even for the musical renditions they found a solution. Mr. Notkiss the secretary, the son of the former Bürgermeister of Pishevits, knew by heart all the words of "Hear, O' Brothers" in Polish and of "There by the Cedars" in German. They came to the conclusion that he would sing them together with his younger brothers and his older sister's son. Even though Notkiss was not a well known student of the kind who would make an impression, it was alright because he was the son of the former Bürgermeister of Pishevits and came from a powerful family. The host got up and rummaged through his books and pulled out one of the pamphlets from *Shachar* that I had loaned him two and half years ago and said, "I've even found a Hebrew poem, 'The Tip of the *Yud*,' by Gordon."

Deixel asked in disbelief, "Gordin? Jacob Gordin wrote poetry in Hebrew? Last winter I happened to meet him at a reception that my academic friends in Lemberg had arranged in his honor. Doctor Shebishifleinu, who had come to greet him on behalf of the cultural association, whispered to me jokingly, "And his beard is fully grown?" When I explained to him that this Gordin was a playwright, the Jewish Shakespeare, Shebishifleinu was forced to change his entire presentation.

Vovi Mundschpiel, who was bored by the discussion of literary matters, said, "I'm surprised that we don't hear any screaming in the town." Our host said, "Wait a while, the workers are still busy in the factory. When they get back from the factory, they'll do their thing. In any event, as long as you stay in my house you need not fear, for my house is made of stone and the window panes are set in iron frames, it's no coincidence that the bank set up residence here."

The time we spent in the home of the head Zionist of Pishevits was pleasant. I became close with Mr. Notkiss. Notkiss is an enlightened man and very well read. He'd read the famous novel *Götz Krafft* in its entirety and relayed to me every amazing feat of that noble, ascetic man. And Notkiss was even a willing reader of Zionist books, such as *Degeneration* by Max Nordau and "Jan Prorok" by Alfred Nossig. As proof of how close we had become, after a week he invited me to come to Pishevits to spend a few days at his house, so that we could arouse each other's idealism and Zionism. All the others that had come with us from Szybusz who were not part of our group, such as the craftsmen and merchants and so on, after having eaten their fill at their relatives in Pishevits, went out to the market hoping that God Himself would find them a bargain and they could recoup their travel expenses.

Chapter Eight
Terror in the City

As we sat drinking tea and partaking of Mrs. Cohen's cakes, we heard the sound of breaking windows. We raised our knives and forks in panic, like the horns of a gored bull about to charge. Suddenly the door opened and a Jew entered the room, looking half dead. And as he entered he doffed his hat as a token of respect for the host and the guests and recounted that the windows of his house had been broken, he had almost been killed and Pesach the Teacher had been dealt murderous blows and might not survive till morning. And have you heard what happened to his daughter in the end? And here he paused slightly, like a man who knows something important and doesn't want to tell it offhandedly, except that he began to fear someone else would beat him to it and blurted out unusually quickly, "The girl was so scared she miscarried her bastard child! Isn't that just like a Socialist floozy for you?" This was said with derision and vindictiveness, as if he wished to humiliate not just her but also all those seated in the house drinking tea and eating cakes and chocolate.

Little Cornelia looked gratefully at the messenger. It seemed to her that this news might cancel the whole business of the recitation. Mrs. Cohen hurriedly sent her off to the bedroom. Dread seized the occupants of the house. "To work, friends!" Mr. Deixel was as pale as a ghost. He was the first to rise to the call. A few of our group didn't budge from their places, for it simply wouldn't do to leave the residents of the home without protection.

As we left we were accosted by a gang of drunken thugs armed with sticks. Before we were able to run away they fell upon us from all directions. We were as good as dead.

At that moment Alexander sprung up from a hidden corner, as Mr. Deixel jumped and hid behind me. Alexander glared at him until I was shaken by what I saw. "I am at your mercy," Deixel's voice was heard. "Go ahead and kill me." Alexander spit in his face and said, "Some other time." And he immediately jumped into the fray and started beating up the drunks until he had dispersed them. Then we breathed a sigh of relief and were encouraged. Even Deixel got hold of himself and began to command the camp like an army officer. The chief of police approached him and asked calmly, "Gentlemen, do you have permission to be standing here on guard?" His words were nothing if not bizarre. What role does permission play when it comes to saving lives? The police chief started up again, "Do you have a written permit from the town clerk to guard the town?" We stood there perplexed and asked, "Who needs a written permit? We've never heard that you need such a permit in Pishevits." The police chief began to holler, "You need it! You need it! Did you come to create mayhem? Son of a bitch, I'm going to handcuff you in a minute. Damn it! Now march!" At that moment two armed policemen appeared restraining Alexander by his arms and they stood him in front of the police chief and said, "When we caught this one, we were shocked. We assumed he was one of ours." The police chief stamped his foot and yelled, "To the jail with this son of a bitch, in handcuffs!"

Quick as an arrow shot from a bow, we fled for our lives. We ran every which way until we arrived safely back at the eating establishment. Thank God no one had been injured. All of the group members who had been with us that afternoon returned, with the exception of those who had stayed behind at the home of Mr. Cohen to defend it. The mixed smells of smoking oil lamps, fish brined and pickled in vinegar and the cigarette smoke of two men who sat at the end of the table with their cards, permeated the entire place. When we entered both men leapt up from their places, but immediately sat back down in disappointment. It was clear that they had been waiting for someone else who had not come.

One of them sighed and said, "Who would have believed that the old Pole Mr. Kortitschnikivitz wouldn't show up today to play cards? For six years he hasn't missed a single card night. Not even Christmas Eve. Here in this very place, he sits in this very empty chair. A dozen oxen couldn't budge him, and yet today he's not here. It's the end of the world. I'm telling you Anti-Semitism is taking over the world." His companion responded, "You see Anti-Semitism everywhere. A clerk calls a Jew a filthy Jew and you immediately cry "Anti-Semitism!" They chase Jewish street peddlers from the market and you right away cry, "Anti-Semitism!" You'd think the nations of the world have nothing else in their world but Anti-Semitism. Tell me, if you please, what do you say about my grandfather, may he rest in peace, whom Mr. Mr. Killerovski found in the forest and made of him a target and shot him with his rifle? Are you going to tell me that this too was Anti-Semitism? And anyway isn't this word Anti-Semitism a recent innovation, and I say that all these things only came about because of the elections, the Zionists and the Socialists. Dr. Bloch and Dr. Davidsohn: they are the ones who have brought trouble on the Jews."

The waitress appeared and said, "The innkeeper's wife is asking whether you gentlemen would prefer to eat the dumplings right away or perhaps you'd like a piece of salted fish first. The innkeeper's wife would like me to tell you that she has both salted fish and pickled fish. The innkeeper's wife says that the pickled fish tickle the palate but even the simpler ones are nice, even though they don't tickle the palate, as the pickled ones are marinated in Turkish pepper and bay leaves and lemon, while the simple only in salt, but they can be prepared with vinegar. Both whet the appetite, but the innkeeper's wife suggests that the gentlemen go with the pickled ones because of their delicacy."

Vovi Mundschpiel asked, "The delicacy of the fish, or the delicacy of the gentlemen?" Deixel chided him, "Don't confuse her, Mundschpiel." Saltzman laid his hand on his belly and said, "But our stomachs are full. How are we going to eat dumplings?" Deixel shouted, "You ordered dumplings, did you not?" And he added, "An honorable man stands by his word." He too made eyes at the waitress and said, "We'll also take the portion of those who aren't here. Appetites will be aroused when the food comes."

Like honorable men who stand by their word, we instructed that the dumplings we had ordered be brought to us, also the portions of those who weren't there. We still remember the innkeeper fondly for pouring us a good Hungarian wine that stimulates digestion and improves the appetite. Deixel drank and was merry. Never in my life had I seen him so cheerful.

The barmaid stood at the bar as she had that afternoon. Mr. Deixel inhaled deeply and offered her a cigarette. She stuck the cigarette in her mouth and smoked it the way men do. Vovi sidled up to her and taught her how to blow smoke through one's nostrils and said, "Interesting things are happening here in your town of Pishevits. I heard it said that an unmarried woman gave birth to twins." She laughed so hard that her belly shook and said, "*Hahaha*, twins he says." The waitress, who initially hadn't ventured to speak up about anything other than the food, approached us and said derisively and vindictively, "Such a snob, she used to be embarrassed to talk to me in the market. And now it seems she buries her head fifteen feet under the ground." The innkeeper puffed up some smoke, pulled the tip of his pipe from his mouth and said, "Socialists, Schmoshalists. It's what a Socialist society is liable to do." His wife added, "May it be the will of the Lord of the Universe for all the Schmoshalists to meet a similar end. And you, my dear husband, I beseech you not to stand where you don't belong. I've told you a thousand times that your place is not at the bar. Take yourself and go. It's not for you, darling, that I hired this barmaid from Lemberg."

The door opened and a limping, drunk man entered the inn. The two Jews were who were sitting at the end of the table with their cards jumped up to greet him and said, "Hooray, here's Mr. Kortitschnikevitz. Welcome, Mr. Kortitschnikevitz! Welcome, Mr. Kortitschnikevitz! Sit down, Your Excellency! Sit down, Your Excellency!"

Mr. Kortitschnikevitz had not been afflicted with the disease of the times and the venom of Anti-Semitism had not poisoned his heart. His heart was as virtuous as ever. Not even a trace of Anti-Semitism could be detected in him. So much to the contrary that after imbibing two pints of spirits, he began to sing a Jewish song:

> *Hot a yud a yudene*
> *Iz zi a groyse tsore tsore*
> *Khapt er zi baym gorgl*
> *Un shlogt mit ir kapore*

> *A Jew he has a wife*
> *She causes so much strife*
> *He grasps her by the throat*
> *And makes from her a scapegoat*

We were all exhausted, but since most of the night had passed without any sleep we agreed to stay awake for the rest of the night. I had not experienced a feeling like this since my days in the study house when I used to stay awake with the adults on the night of *Hoshana Rabba*. The night passed peacefully. Outside of two or three windows being broken, the hand of the enemy did not touch the Jews. When morning dawned, we went out for a breath of air. The blinds were open. The world was ready to resume its course.

Chapter Nine

An Unattended Corpse, *or*
Fortunate Is the Father

A morning breeze blew. The trees gave off a scent of dew. The night guard awoke from his sleep and headed home. The cows went out to pasture in the field. Youths stood outside washing their faces at the well. A door opened and women went out to the market to buy food staples and men went to say the morning prayers.

The town beadle came out and stood in the midst of the marketplace and called out, "An unattended corpse, an unattended corpse!" Asked one person in alarm, "Who died? Who died?" The beadle answered him, "No one died here." "Then why are you calling out 'an unattended corpse'?" he asked. He responded, "He was killed." Who had been killed? Pesach the Teacher had been killed. The Jew lowered his head, sighed and said, "Blessed be the True Judge."

One woman passing through stopped and said, "I hear that you're discussing Pesach. And it's so horrible that just last Sabbath eve he was drinking '*L'Chaim! To life!*' with the whole study house and today he lies dead. Oh and alas to that kind of drinking. There in the study house he drank on behalf of his chaste daughter Miss Peshi Shaindel who had taken ill with a sickness that the doctor called 'morning sickness,' and it never had been before among the Hasids that such an illness even existed, and they said a blessing asking God to send her a complete and speedy recovery from this new malady. What an impertinent one, she! Fortunate is the father who didn't merit learning the meaning of that illness."

An old porter walked bent over, the purification board on his back. The Jew whom I had encountered yesterday in Mr. Levi Cohen's house tapped me on the shoulder and said, "Didn't I tell you that I couldn't guarantee that he'd live till morning? Indeed, I could have said that he would surely die but I didn't want to ask for trouble. Now I must run to the synagogue – it's Monday, the day of reading the Torah and I have to say the blessing thanking God for deliverance." Vovi Mundschpiel said "The blessing for deliverance for not having been infected by this new disease 'morning sickness.'"

We drank coffee and ate breakfast. Vovi Mundschpiel yawned and said, "Thank God that the train is departing for Szybusz. The only reason Pishevits was put on earth was for getting bored with its barmaid. Did you hear Peppy Miller is scheduled to come to Szybusz?" "No," some of our group responded with doubtful anticipation. Vovi said, "Oberschenkil already swore to me that he has invited her to come." One of the group winked and said, "Now that's a woman." His friend added, "And when she braids herself ear locks and wears Hasidic garb, she looks totally like a Hasid." Vovi Mundschpiel lowered himself, raised one shoulder, twirled his fingers where his sidelocks would have been and began to make up a poem:

> *Ich bin ein Chasid'l*
> *Mit tzvay langeh pay'es*
> *Dray ich mein s'pudikil*
> *Oon zog in himmel day'es*
>
> *I am a little Hasid*
> *With long curls on each side*
> *I spin my tall fur hat*
> *And importune the sky*

I dance a little Hasid hop
And then God I implore you:
Why would you ever give a head
To a man who's not a Jew?

Well, a trusty pair of hands
A Gentile surely needs
For stones he has to carry
And he digs the earth for weeds

Also to a pair of legs
I harbor no objection
But what good's a head for a Gentile?
That's my burning question

Now, calm yourself dear child
He says with great affection
Don't be so upset with me
I'll answer now your question

By my tallis and my kittel
I will swear to you on that
The reason Esau has a head
Is so he'll buy from you a hat

Veixel yelled out, "What impertinence! Now that even Dr. Davidsohn speaks highly of the Hasids, this one comes along and makes fun of them."

Veixel was not well liked by us, but there was a bit of truth in what he said.

We found the rest of our clan at the train station. Even Cohen and Notkiss had come to give us a proper send-off. Some exchanged pleasantries saying, "This was a nice evening we had." And others responded, "Yes, an exceedingly nice evening." And some were yawning so hard it looked like the skin on their faces was about to split open. We asked our friends who arrived to join up with us, "And what did you occupy yourselves with all night?" "With a deck of cards," they replied. Faivel Karkafta said, "I won twenty kreutzers" and then grew silent in the manner of silence that implied, "If I were not so modest, I would tell you much more." Notkiss said, "And half of it he donated to the national fund."

Chapter Ten
Of Language and of Art

Veixel repeated what Deixel had said, "Every cloud has a silver lining. We came to get beaten up and we ended up organizing a ball." Deixel stretched out leisurely on the bench, let out a grunt and said, "A ball." This grunting was by way of a dismissal of the ball's significance and an opening for conversation. One of the group members began by saying, "Mr. Cohen deserves to be supported in his Zionist work." Said another, "Quite a feast his wife set out for us." And a third added, "My heart went out to little Cornelia." A fourth chimed in, "You remember that cluster of grapes on the table? I swear I almost reached out to pluck one." Deixel said, "There is an important axiom in the art world, namely that something artificial has to look lifelike, while something that is real has to look artificial." I asked Mr. Deixel, "Such as?" Mr. Deixel thought about this deeply and replied, "Such as…" Suddenly, he slapped me on the knee and said, "Such as Lilien. Have you seen his painting of the kabbalist? Literally like a photograph." How delightful was Deixel's discourse, as he knew how to give just the right amount of attention to each and every topic, and I still regret that our friends interrupted him with trivialities and that I didn't have a chance to hear all of Mr. Deixel's views about art.

What were our friends focused on? Those dumplings! There were those who said that Mrs. Cohen's dumplings were better than those at the inn and others that said, "The gall of villagers! The entire time the innkeeper prevailed upon us to eat as if he had been giving us food for free, yet at the end he stood there and demanded two kreutzers for every dumpling that we'd consumed." But Vovi Mundschpiel defended the innkeeper saying, "Even villagers have to make a living. It's not every day that a miracle occurs and guests arrive in Pishevits. But where is the Russian? Where is Alexander?" Someone responded and said, "For sure he will stay behind until after the burial, in order to pay his last respects to his father-in-law."

"Why, is he married?"

"What else, then? Was Peshi Shaindel impregnated by the holy spirit?"

Yaakov Shimshon, the son of the ritual slaughterer, whispered to me, "I found in the *Sefer HaYuhasin* the story of Pope Joan, a learned woman who dressed in men's clothing and was a pope, and no one realized she was a woman until one day while passing through the marketplace during a papal holiday procession she gave birth. What do you say to that?" I said to him, "What can I say?" He said to me, "Why don't you ask the student Deixel what's written in the Christian books on this topic?" Yaakov Shimshon, the son of the ritual slaughterer, had already been out of the study house six months, but still hadn't particularly warmed up to our student friends.

Someone began and said, "If not for Alexander, we would have been severely beaten. Where had he been hiding at that moment? Did you notice how it was as if he had come out of nowhere? Alone he stood his ground against many Gentiles." Said Veixel, "What of it? He's still used to this from Russia." And as he spoke he was looking at Mr. Deixel. Deixel didn't respond to him with the same affectionate smile that generally graced his lips. Yaakov Shimshon, the son of the ritual slaughterer, said, "It's customary to call someone named Alexander, Sander or Zusha, but this one is not called by any nicknames. It seems that over in Russia Alexanders are called Alexander." Said Henrik Salzmander, "All Russians are fierce. Did you see his strength? Did you see how he stood up to them?" Veixel replied, "That's not strength, that's courage. And if you push me, I'll say that even courage was not involved. I mean you heard the police say when they had captured him they'd thought he was one of them, and if he'd really been brave he could have pretended to be a Gentile. It is told about Rinaldo Rinaldini that one time the kingdom announced that a reward would be granted to anyone who caught him. One guy caught him and brought him to the police. What did Rinaldo Rinaldini do? He placed his hand on the shoulder of the guy who'd caught him and said to the police, 'Here I present to you Rinaldo Rinaldini.' And thus he won the reward the kingdom had offered for his own capture. Now that's courage!" Vovi Mundschpiel said, "It's worrisome that they might return him to Russia and exile him to Siberia." An unbearable and cruel silence reigned suddenly in the train. I don't know what came over me, but my heart suddenly went limp, melting in fear.

Veixel said, "He didn't have to jump in. It was of his own doing. Had he not provoked the rioters, he'd be sitting here in the train returning with us to Szybusz."

I turned away from all of my friends and wandered among the rest of the passengers in the car. Some of them sat on benches filled with wares, while others of them rolled cigarettes and told stories to entertain themselves. Said one shopkeeper to his train companion, "I'm dying to know who invented the railroad." The other responded, "What's the point in wondering? Look it up in the almanac. You'll even find the year there." The shopkeeper came back, "Was it Columbus?" His friend replied, "It's possible." The other said, "In any event, it's a wondrous thing that a man can move his bowels in Pishevits and say the bathroom blessing in Szybusz."

After two hours of traveling, the train arrived in Szybusz. My mother buried her face in my neck weeping and smothering me with kisses and said, "My son, my son, where have you been, my son?" From the surrounding houses sounds of weeping and kissing were heard. "This new generation doesn't have God in their hearts. They up and leave their mothers and put their lives in jeopardy." My father came from the store, greeted me and said, "Once again you've given up a day of Torah study." I retorted, "All of Pishevits was facing danger." He said to me, "While you were in Pishevits did you even visit the Rabbi?" Mother said, "Wash your hands, my son, and eat." My father shook his head sadly and said to her, "Woe to him if he does everything that you say." Mother didn't pay heed to father's words and said, "Where is the fresh egg?" My little sister held the egg in her gaze. My other sister teased her and said, "Why does a young man who learns Torah rub his eyes with a fresh egg to get them used to the Torah, little one, why?" Mother added, "Hush, little ones, and don't reveal to him what I have prepared for him as a punishment for worrying his mother." "My dear mother, even if you don't tell me what you cooked for me, the aroma of the dish has already revealed itself."

Chapter Eleven
Strife Among Brothers

There was news in Szybusz. We'd been gone all of one day from our town and momentous events had taken place. The prior day Mrs. Dr. Zilberman, the wife of Dr. Zilberman, had been reading aloud a chapter in Raumer's book about girls' education when she slipped up on a word that can have two meanings. What did the student Gold do? The student Gold cried out, "Encore!" – in other words, he urged her to repeat her mistake. And the scholars of Szybusz determined that this was shameful. Gold had committed two offenses. For one thing, the word "encore" is only appropriately used in the theater world, so if he had said "encore," it suggested that he regarded the honored speaker as an actress. Secondly, if a civilized man hears a woman getting mixed up over a word that can have two meanings, it behooves him to pretend he didn't hear it. As the proverb goes, "you can't make a silk purse out a sow's ear." Even though he's a student, he still comes from a line of butchers. Based on that offense, Zilber the apothecary challenged Gold to a duel to the death. And Mr. Zilber had already sent him his second. Gold's father was screaming and said, "I shall go in your place, my son! I will immediately take a hatchet and break his bones! Like a slaughtered calf I will lay him in front of you here on the chopping block of the butcher shop!" Wretched Gold! Who knew if his father might not do something at odds with convention? Mr. Gold said to his father, "Father, you're not the one whose honor is to be satisfied." Father Gold said, "Meaning?" Mr. Gold said, "I've already told you a thousand times that you do not have permission to stand for the duel." Father Gold replied, "Even if in your estimation I'm forbidden to be killed, I can still kill. I'm going to immediately bring him down like a young steer, right here on this chopping block of the butcher shop!"

Meanwhile Mrs. Zilber, the mother of apothecary Zilber, had come to the butcher shop to buy meat. Mother Gold stood and screamed at her, "You want to kill my son! I swear on your life that yours will be killed first! A strange death will befall you and your son. I swear on your life, my grandsons will dance on your graves! No apothecary has yet been buried in our cemetery. Daughters of Szybusz go out and behold the scalp of the apothecary. I swear that his face is like a moist hemorrhoid." And Mother Gold did not calm down until she had thrown a cow's stomach in Mrs. Zilber's face. Mrs. Zilber wiped her face and said, "Butcheress, you're lucky that cow's stomach didn't soil my dress. I swear you would have paid for the damage."

Zilber was walking tall. An expression of seriousness adorned his face and a spirit of bravery floated on his lips. And he got up early to be there when Mr. Dovidzeni, the president of the sports club, opened up so that he could solicit advice about weapons. Everywhere that you found Zilber's seriousness there you also found his smile. Mrs. Zilberman and also Steffi Oberschenkil, Gold's fiancée, wrote him letters, the kind of scented letters that are written on thick paper in long envelopes with gilded edges. But the joy was not complete, with him turning his head every so often and looking over his shoulder lest Gold's parents try and attack him. Those creatures do not abide by the rules of satisfaction.

Chapter Twelve

The Importance of Mrs. Zilberman
and Her Husband Dr. Zilberman

Mrs. Zilberman, the wife of Dr. Zilberman, was a short woman, a little on the heavy side, she had the trace of a beard and her lips were compressed together. Such a sense of energy emanated from her face that all who encountered her knew immediately that she possessed an extraordinary spirit and that it would be wrong to show her even an iota of disrespect. She brought in a dowry of twenty thousand to her husband. The size of this dowry had the risk of devaluing Mrs. Zilberman's honor because after all the rest of the doctors in Szybusz took wives with dowries of only fifteen thousand gulden, but it would appear that her father could not get rid of her unless he spent twenty thousand on her. But it was not so. On the contrary Zilberman actually got a small dowry. And what caused Zilberman to give up so much? The year he married his wife the gulden had been taken out of circulation and replaced with the krone. At first, when a person said twenty thousand it was understood that he meant twenty thousand gulden, but when they began to use the krone coin, which was half a gulden, the world was divided. The young did their calculations in kroner, while the older ones did so in gulden. Our town, which is not big on innovation, did its calculations according to the standard that had prevailed before the gulden had exited the market. But Mrs. Zilberman's father, who was a resident of Lemberg and a modern man who adapted himself to the times, accepted the latest version of matters and when he said twenty thousand he meant twenty thousand kroner. I have no idea whether Zilberman understood that his father-in-law was talking about twenty thousand kroner, which was a mere was ten thousand gulden, and was satisfied with what everyone else was thinking, or whether even he himself was deceived. In any event, we never heard that he had taken revenge upon his wife, rather we heard that peace had reigned between them. Peshi Shaindel, who was their housemaid, even used to brag that they lived together like a pair of turtledoves.

Dr. Zilberman was the son of a poor family. His father had been a part-time landlord and a part-time butcher. His garb was like that of any respectable Jew in Szybusz, a velvet hat on his head and a proper overcoat over, with a sash tied around his waist. Most of the day he would sit at the study house reading all types of religious texts, while his wife sat at the butcher shop taking pride in her husband. Once a day he would go out to the market and assist her with her dealings and when he'd enter the butcher shop would tuck his coattails into his sash and work with her as a butcher and she would chide him affectionately saying, "How disgraceful for a Torah scholar to undertake such lowly work" and would raise her voice so that the neighborhood women would hear that this learned one was not ashamed of her and what's more would even plunge into butcher's work with her. And he would do his work calmly and would pay no attention to her chiding and the neighbors would place their hands on their bellies under their aprons and say about him, "From the midriff up he is a proper fellow and from the midriff down he's a butcher."

Dr. Zilberman was his father and mother's only child. His father and mother doted on him and spoiled him in every which way. While he was still immersed in love and being spoiled as an only child, his mother died and before he was even nine years old his father remarried. From this time on he pulled back from his son because his new wife was a shopkeeper who took pride in her shop and the butcheress's son reminded her of the disgrace of both the butcheress and her husband. So that the townsfolk wouldn't tittle-tattle "wicked step-mother" behind her back she would be careful not to leave obvious marks on the boy when she beat him, rather she would hit him in the belly or swipe him in the ribs. If it were not for his aunt in Lemberg, he would have ended up like all of the other poor orphans in our town.

This aunt, his mother's sister, was a maidservant in the home of a wealthy old man in Lemberg. After she had been in his service for most of her life, he married her and enabled her to do acts of charity and kindness for her poor relatives. Every year when she would visit the graves of her ancestors in Szybusz she would bring her brother-in-law clothing that the "old man" had discarded but was still as good as new, and she would have new clothes made for the child – that is, little Zilberman whom she called her only child – and would bring him excellent gifts such as peanuts which are called "Moses Nuts" and all sorts of other things that weren't known in our town and which would endear him to his school friends. She would also pay for his tuition so that he would learn Torah and become a Torah scholar, and after a hundred and twenty years would remember her soul by reciting the Mourner's Kaddish and a chapter of Mishnah. And she already had inquired of the rabbinical judge as to whether it would be permissible for him to recite the Kaddish for her while his own parents were still living, inasmuch as the wretched one was convinced she would die first. Since her sister's death preceded hers she said, "I tempted fate and hastened her death by anticipating the Mourner's Kaddish." Sometime later, when she came to erect a headstone at her sister's grave, she saw her "only child" mired in his suffering and wept with him about his troubles until she mounted the carriage to return to Lemberg and the orphan ran behind her crying, "Auntie, Auntie!" The butcheress Gold pointed the orphan towards the carriage and said, "Get on there, you fool. Get on!" His aunt pulled him by the hand and said, "Sit and come with me to Lemberg." This was said abruptly and harshly so that he didn't know whether to be happy or sad about the trip. When she got to Lemberg and told her husband everything that had transpired, the old man patted the child's cheeks and gave him room and board in his house and enrolled him in school so he could learn reading and writing.

Zilberman studied in sadness, for he was in fear of being sent back to Szybusz. In reality, he had nothing to be afraid of as his aunt had already made up her mind not to return the orphan to the deadly one in Szybusz and the old man had agreed with her. It was difficult for the old man to take his shoes off. An old man eats little and his belly fills up quickly. He was hunched over from age and yet he couldn't bend over; indeed when he put his shoe into the shoe extractor it would not come off. Either he would lose strength in his hand or the extractor would get damaged. Old age is difficult and especially removing shoes for an old man. He would joke around say, "Children, try not to experience old age." One time the orphan noticed the old man standing at the shoe extractor, struggling to remove his shoes, and he jumped to his aid and pulled off the shoes for him. The old man sang the boy's praises that entire day. "Here I am standing and sweating in front of that shoe extractor, and the device is either sitting there immovable as a stone or it moves with me, but the shoe doesn't budge a hair's breadth. And as I'm standing there the little one grabs my feet, immediately I feel a spring breeze, I peer down and realize that I'm standing shoeless. This little one has accomplished in a moment what the extractor and I couldn't manage in half an hour." That entire night the old man lay awake, reminding himself of all the details of the event. And even though he'd been awake the whole night, he awoke refreshed. And even though he'd resigned himself to having to wear slippers like all the elderly, now he could continue to wear leather shoes until a hundred and twenty years old. From here on in, the boy would take off his shoes for him all the time. The wooden extractor still remained in its place, but was never used. The little one had inherited its job and was destined to share in the old man's inheritance.

Not many years passed before the old man went to meet his maker and left behind both money and movables that sufficed for Zilberman to study worry-free until he had completed medical school. When he had received his physician's license he returned to

Szybusz and began treating patients, and since he had not been in Szybusz all of those years and since when he returned he did so as a doctor, they treated him with the respect they would commonly afford to non-Szybuszites. And his stature and his countenance and his demeanor all stood him in good stead, for he was of good height, had a pleasing appearance and was personable. And he had the ability to converse with people easily and would respond to everyone's greetings, even those of children. Truly they said that the greetings of Dr. Zilberman were akin to being bestowed a kindness, as this was how he responded: he would transfer his cigarette from his right hand to his left and raise his right hand calmly to his head, lifting his hat and waving it slightly, and then replacing it on his head. He never got involved with either politics or town affairs and wasn't exceptional at anything, unlike all the other doctors in Szybusz, each and every one of whom excelled in his own eccentricity. But it was in his lack of remarkability that he was remarkable.

In contrast to that, his wife was involved in community affairs and founded a women's society in Szybusz, called the "Ruth Sisterhood." At first all of Szybusz's jokesters would make jokes at her expense, saying that it is strange for women to form societies. It didn't take long for these jesters to be silenced, for their daughters found there a warm and welcoming corner, and furthermore they brought with them their older sisters who had given up on marriage due to their advanced age and were ashamed to show their faces in public. And when the winter days came and the dark evenings would drag on and boredom would set in, they would gather themselves at the "Ruth" house. It was warm inside and magazines were spread out on the tables and students would congregate there and the conversations were pleasant, and because this society was more cultural than political even students from wealthy homes used to come there, students who were drawn to Socialism and would denigrate Zionism as a movement of the bourgeoisie.

In particular, Mrs. Zilberman is worthy of praise inasmuch as she initiated the presentation of lectures on history and literature. Even she herself would lecture from time to time and when she would do so, the hall would be packed. Anyone who hasn't heard Mrs. Zilberman when she is concluding her lecture has not witnessed a woman being honored, for the entire audience would applaud her, shake her hand and shower her with words of praise and gratitude. And surely one has to wonder about Mr. Gold who had treated her so shabbily.

Chapter Thirteen

Gold and Zilber, as the Story Goes

This whole episode troubled me greatly, especially as they were both my dear friends and if not dear friends, then surely acquaintances. I was reminded about the time they found me at the Zionist society, reading, and invited me to go for a walk with them, and during our walk they told me that Mrs. Zilberman had asked them to give a lecture to the "Ruth Sisterhood" but that they still didn't know what they were going to speak about. Zilber wanted to speak about Jewish art, while Gold wanted to speak about Jewish music, except that Deixel wasn't loaning out his copies of "*Ost und West*" and they were unable to come up with any other original themes. I said to them, "But after all you know Polish and have access to their history books, so perhaps you could lecture about the history of the Jews in Poland." But they did not agree. Mr. Zilber said, "If I speak about the times of the Jews in Poland, I'll have to mention what that priest sermonized about in their church last week and my talk will be found to be unscholarly." And Mr. Gold said, "What is there to tell about the history of the Jews in Poland? Everyone who studied Polish history in high school learned about the Jews in Poland one way or another." And he continued, "We want current, modern themes."

It was then that I suggested to them that they speak about Hebrew and about Yiddish. There is nothing more current. They immediately took out their notepads and began peppering me with questions. And still they had not determined which one of them would talk about Hebrew and which about Yiddish until I just settled it for them, saying that Zilber would talk about Yiddish and Gold about Hebrew" – except that they changed it around, with Zilber speaking about Hebrew and Gold about Yiddish.

Because of the biblical episode of Yoav and Shimmi, I was very careful to pronounce for them with exactitude the name of each writer, whether Hebrew or Yiddish, and similarly all of the names of their poems, stories, plays, articles and pseudonyms. And so they wouldn't pronounce anything wrong, they spelled it all out in transliteration in their notepads.

If you see two people taunting each other, you can be sure there was already a shred of resentment in their hearts from day one. Now, at the time of the duel, I recalled that the seeds of their hatred had already begun to blossom on the evenings of their lectures, when they debated as to whether Hebrew or Yiddish was more important. Gold, who had been enlisted as the patron of Yiddish, maintained that Yiddish literature was the essence of Zionism. That were it not for Morris Rosenfeld and Sholem Asch whose works were translated into German no cultured person would pay attention to Yiddish, but now that their works had been translated into German all the Western pundits turn to Yiddish and therefore no Jew is ashamed to speak it, and one finds that that it is Yiddish that strengthens nationalism and unites hearts. And not only that but also that because Yiddish is a new language without all the strange traditions of the holy tongue it's possible to make it progressive so that it won't be claimed that the Jews are reactionaries, and thus the entirety of our existence depends on Yiddish. Zilber, who had been enlisted as the patron of Hebrew, said that it was not so, but exactly the opposite. Inasmuch as Hebrew is not a living language like all the others but rather a language of the future to come, it contains within it the symbol of our resurrection, a psalm of praise for the coming days when we will be a living nation like all others. For that reason we must fortify the Hebrew language, as language is a core factor in the life of every nation, all the more so as Hebrew is a kind of bridge between the glowing future and the lofty past. The same lofty past that gave us Moses and Aaron and Judah Halevi, in whose honor Heine composed a great poem and thus it is written in his poem: "My beloved, leave aside the theater and the concerts and learn Hebrew."

And it might even be that I bear the blame for the war between the two of them, and perhaps not just me but also Reuben Brainin. Brainin and me, how so? The same day that Gold and Zilber invited me to take a walk with them, I had been reading an article about a newly discovered Yiddish poet. Even though this poet had written but three poems, the article's author had said that nevertheless it was within his power to bring about a revolution in poetry. And before I had read these things I'd been reading Brainin's article on Y. L. Gordon and because these things had been written in *HaShiloah* under the signature of a modern writer I had shown them to Gold and Zilber, and from them Zilber had acquired the horns with which to gore Hebrew poetry and prove that it is worthless and he was reminded to praise the new Yiddish writer who was destined to bring about a revolution in the world of poetry, until the hearts of all the ladies who were listening were filled with fervor. Especially inflamed was the heart of one Miss Steffi Oberschenkil who had previously set her eyes on Gold. Knowing in my heart that I had caused the war between the two of them, because but for my having given advice to Mr. Zilber and Mr. Gold to lecture on Hebrew and Yiddish they wouldn't have done so, my conscience was bothering me without end, so I determined that I would go and talk to them to see if I couldn't encourage them to leave this whole unfortunate business behind.

A Chapter Within a Chapter
Gold in and of Himself

Ｉt would have been fitting for me to go to Zilber first, inasmuch as
he was the instigator. If so, why did I go to Gold first? Because the
one who was offended is always closer to the heart than is the one
who committed the offense.

Gold stood alone in the middle of the room facing the mirror
holding a rolling pin which he was swinging back and forth, and soon
enough he hit the mirror and almost shattered it out of the hostility
simmering within him. When he saw me he ran up and wept upon my
neck and said, "Why would I want to live while she is writing letters to
him?" Even though he didn't specify their names I understood on my
own that "she" referred to Miss Oberschenkil, whilst "him" meant Zilber.
And Gold went on crying like that and saying, "In the prime of my life
will I descend into hell and here I had said I would surely do something for our people. Lying on the table is my lecture on Yiddish that I
had said I would send to the *Voskhod* but I have no strength to recopy
it, after all for whom do I toil? Truly the Polish writer got it right:

> *Cudze chwalicie*   *Swego nie znacie,*
> *Sami nie wiecie*   *Co posiadacie.*

The work of others do you laud,
Yet you know not that of your own,
You yourselves know not what you have.

Continuation:
Zilber in and of Himself

I did not find Zilber at home. His father told me he had gone to the club, while his mother told me he had gone to see the wife of Doctor Zilberman and his sister hinted that he was at Steffi Oberschenkil's. In the end I found him strolling in the marketplace with Mr. Dovidzeni.

Mr. Dovidzeni, the Polish leader of the gymnastics club in Szybusz, was wearing a long black cloak over his shoulders, its two sleeves were fluttering in the wind, and he was always raising his two arms and spreading them out this way and that like someone swimming in the river. He was walking on the sidewalk with Zilber alongside him, but because Dovidzeni kept stretching out his arms while talking Zilber kept getting knocked into the road and having to get back up onto the sidewalk. And he would get pushed into the road again and scurry between the sidewalk and the road and the road to the sidewalk. I greeted him and he didn't answer me. I greeted him once again and he greeted me Zilberman-style, while having one foot on the sidewalk and the other in the roadway. Nonetheless, I followed after him so that when he was done with Mr. Dovidzeni I'd be able to speak with him. In this way I unintentionally overheard their conversation.

Mr. Dovidzeni was strolling and saying, "Oberschenkil's daughter is a lovely young Jewess. In general all of the young Jewesses are lovely and of brilliant intellect, but I can't stand Jews. When a Jew passes by my house my dog immediately grabs him by his clothing and bites his flesh. My dogs are trained and they don't bark while doing their work, just hold the garment and bite the flesh. Oh boy! But when it comes to Jewesses, the dogs don't do them any real harm. The Lord God gave dogs wisdom. I behave kindly to Jewesses and this is what I say to them: 'My whole garden is open to you, sweet does,' and not only that but I also like to bounce them on my knee. Damn them, they all run away from me. Jews are faithless, they are all cheats. And your Alterel is the biggest cheat of all. Look what happened: his fellow Jews wanted to prevent him from building his house, because a Jew begrudges the enjoyment of others, and if not for the Baron Pitshinski who went to the city and told the builders to build, Alterel wouldn't have standing in the world and yet in the end he went and deceived Pitshvinski's son. When the younger baron desired a proper daughter of Israel for himself and said to your Alterel, 'Now I want a proper daughter of Israel' what did your Alterel do? He took a Polish maid who served among the Jews and knew the Jewish language, dressed her in Jewish garb and brought her before him, and whispered that she was a butcher's daughter. She found favor in his eyes immediately and the next day he praised her as the most modest woman he had ever seen. Not long afterwards he killed himself. There are those who say he killed himself out of shame when he found out that a Jew had deceived him and there are those who say it was because he had caught some serious, incurable diseases from her. And what did Alterel say to the elder baron when the latter rebuked him saying, 'This is how you pay me back for all the favors I did for you over the years?' Alterel cried before him and said, 'My enlightened lord, how could I have known that the provincial officer had had his way with her first.' You're asking me, Mr. Apothecary, what kind of weapon is appropriate for that contemptible Zilber - *umm*, for Gold I meant to say? Take a revolver of six bullets. Boom, boom, and you'll be rid of your enemy and the world will be rid of one more Jew."

When I heard this I ran as fast as my legs would take me to Deixel. After all, he is the head of the student Zionist organization in Szybusz and the student Zionists are obliged to heed his word and I went to ask him to take any action necessary in order to prevent Zilber from taking action.

Deixel sat reading "*Ost und West.*" He was already fed up with propaganda speeches and was preparing an artistic speech for the Pishevits ball. "My friend," said Deixel, "a capable orator can accomplish more with an artistic speech than with any propaganda sermon. Perhaps you've heard, my friend, that D'Annunzio was seeking election to the legislature so he stood and gave a speech on the differences between epic and lyrical poetry and was elected unanimously. You might think that the voters were learned, but you should know that they couldn't even read or write. Similarly, my dear friend Shebishifleinu spoke on Hanukkah and half of his speech came from *The Sunken Bell* by Gerhart Hauptmann and his words made quite an impression."

Deixel's words were very nice and worth listening to, except that at that moment I was envisioning Gold writhing on the ground, bleeding to death. I said to myself, "A Jew is about to be killed and we're occupied with poetry." Deixel stood, put his hand on my shoulder and said, "I had almost forgotten about this entire business. New disputes consign the older ones to oblivion. Have you ever heard in your life about the differences between Sephardic and Ashkenazic pronunciation? Didn't you tell me that the Ashkenazi Jews pray in the Ashkenazic tradition and the Hasids pray in the Sephardic tradition, and to what do you attribute the phenomenon that both the Hasids and the Ashkenazim are united in their objection to Sephardic pronunciation?"

I stood there staring at Deixel in astonishment. Here I was pleading with him that the blood of his friend was about to be shed and he was lecturing about finer points in pronunciation. Mr. Deixel knew what was in my heart and he said, "Once again a dispute has broken out in town on account of the school. The teachers want the Sephardic pronunciation to be used and the parents want the Ashkenazic pronunciation and the entire town is raising a ruckus like it's the end of the world. Jews can't live without arguing. Tell me please, if you would, what the difference is between this pronunciation and the other and we'll go to the meeting." Before I had the chance to finish expounding on the distinctions between the forms of pronunciation, the school caretaker arrived and told us that the entire assembly had already gone into the meeting. Mr. Deixel grabbed me by the arm and said, "Come with me, my friend."

May the same thing never befall you. So much effort had been expended by us on founding this Hebrew school. So many teachers we had brought in who had fallen upon hard times and we didn't notice their extreme distress when they came imploring us that their children had nothing to eat, and already we had merited seeing the results of our labor with the chattering of Hebrew in the town squares. Little girls would say to their friends, "*Tsafra tava! Ramsha tava!*" And now the school was on the verge of being destroyed, God forbid, due to matters of pronunciation. Deixel was right when he said, "New disputes consign the older ones to oblivion."

Chapter Fourteen

About The Wars and Incontrovertible
Evidence That I Was Not Exaggerating
When I Said My Dear Friend
Mr. Deixel is Extremely Important

Such a huge assembly had not been seen in Szybusz since the last elections. Had I not come with Sigmund Deixel I would have been left outside.

A learned elderly householder, a scholar who had been one of the founders of the school, stood on the dais with his eyes closed, explaining the whole issue of the pronunciations. The elderly one was saying, "So said the sage the Ya'avetz…" The school director interrupted him loudly, "If you don't mind, sir, yours are but the words of a reactionary. From whom are you adducing proof, from Ze'ev Yavetz who is already known to be religious and conservative? It is a disgrace to a progressive institute like this Hebrew school to mention his name." The elderly one responded, "Even the sage Rabbi Jacob Emden, may his memory be a blessing, who favors Sephardic pronunciation differs on several grounds. First and foremost, the Ya'avetz says…" At that moment, Veixel whispered to the chair that

Deixel had arrived. The committee head rang a bell to silence him and the elderly one got mixed up in the middle of his speech and asked, "Who's here?" Immediately from all sides people began to cry out, "Deixel's here! Deixel's here!" Right away they made room for him to pass through to mount the dais and everyone was applauding in his honor and calling out, "Hooray, hooray! Deixel's going to speak!" The committee head rang the bell once again, wiped his brow and shouted, "Hush!" Deixel began, "Gentlemen, you have called for me and I have come. But who am I to express my opinion on such weighty matters. To my shame and my disgrace I have focused all of my attention only on foreign languages, on Polish and German and Latin and Greek and French and Ruthenian and, if you will permit me, also on the language of Great Britain, a land about which it can rightly be said that the sun never sets upon her, a land whose inhabitants eat fresh food all the days of the year, a land that wanted to give Uganda to our great leader Theodore Herzl, except that thanks to Ussishkin and his friends, the heroes of Kharkov, we are still wandering among the Gentiles like Ahasver, the eternal wandering Jew." And here Mr. Deixel swallowed a sip of water and the entire audience rejoined, "Boo to you, Kharkov! Boo to you, heroes of Kharkov!"

Someone from the audience said, "It is not in keeping with parliamentary procedure to abuse people in their absence." His friend said to him, "Maybe I should go and drag them by their beards and bring them here?" A third one said, "Do they even have beards?" He responded, "If not, then by their moustaches." Shimshon Yaakov the son of the ritual slaughterer said, "Some of them do have beards. With my own eyes I've seen a drawing of a Zionist who had a beard." Said Faivel Karkafta, "May their names be blotted out, they oppose Herzl, but they imitate his beard like an ape. Even our Dr. Davidsohn is growing himself a beard."

Deixel wiped his mouth and said, "My own vineyard I have not kept. Nevertheless, as an outsider who is familiar with the ways of the cultured nations regarding their languages I will surely announce that the teacher has prevailed. Indeed, gentlemen, the teacher has prevailed as only a teacher can. Therefore, we must rely on the knowledge of our honored teacher..." (At this point the principal turned red and whispered in his ear, "he's the director.") "Yes, yes," continued Deixel, "the *director* of the Hebrew Institute."

The student Deixel finished speaking to a round of loud applause and the teacher from the Hebrew Institute had won. And the victory was yet not complete when the teacher opened up a Hebrew textbook and said, "Here!" And he looked at his antagonists with such scorn and contempt that his face was distorted in disgust.

The committee members asked the teacher, "What are you showing us here?" He answered them, "I said it once and I'm not repeating myself." They bent their heads towards the textbook and he took a pencil from behind his ear and thrust it into the book like a teacher of young children pointing out letters and shouted, "Clearly the author of the textbook knows that the Sephardic pronunciation is correct. He's right and it's not worthwhile for me to argue with you." One of the committee said, "It never occurred to me until now." The doctor said to him, "Columbus's detractors also said that about the matter of the egg, as it is known." At that moment the committee members cast their faces downward towards the ground and were silent and the audience clapped and called out, "Hooray, hooray, hooray! The teacher has won! The teacher has won!"

Chapter Fifteen

The Author Elaborates On His Trip to Pishevits and Why He Didn't Go Immediately

Deixel is true to his word. And he'd already set with Mr. Levi Cohen a time for the Pishevits ball and in honor of the ball had ordered portraits of our great leaders and of the farming settlements in the Land of Israel and also the correct version of the national anthem. And already Veixel was busy making many copies, so that the Zionists of Pishevits would not get tripped up while singing it.

At that time the secretary, Mr. Notkiss, had sent me Nordau's *Degeneration* so that I could get it bound and he sent a note with the book inviting me to come see him in Pishevits, because with a lack of friends the mind will degenerate. Even Deixel was trying to persuade me to go, because Pishevits had never been fortunate enough to have a Zionist ball and therefore every loyal Zionist must come to Pishevits and afterwards report every detail of the affair of the ball in all of our newspapers.

Before going to Pishevits, I went to the bookbinder to collect the *Degeneration* book to bring it to Notkiss. When I saw what a nice job the bookbinder had done, I resolved to give him some of my own books for binding. I was reminded of Mendele's *Mare* which I had loaned to Alexander and I went to see him at the blacksmith's to retrieve my book, but I did not find Alexander.

The blacksmith's shop was on the outskirts of the town where the roads diverged and lead to the villages. The small homes, most of which resemble village houses, and the small children running around barefoot in the grass and climbing trees brought to mind the rural life in the Land of Israel, as I pictured it in my head in those days. At that same moment, I emitted a heartfelt groan, "Master of the Universe, when are you going to bring me up to the Land of Israel?"

I asked the blacksmith, "Where is Alexander?" The blacksmith said to me, "I myself have also been wondering where he is." I said to him, "Is he not here?" He said to me, "He is not here." I asked him, "Where did he go?" He said, "He went to Pishevits." I asked him, "When did he go to Pishevits?" He said to me, "The same day that your Dr. Davidsohn left." I said to him, "And he hasn't come back?" "He didn't come back." At that moment, I said to myself, "Woe is me. He's still incarcerated," and I returned to town, trembling and desolate, not knowing what to do. To go to Deixel was out of the question because he was preoccupied with his speech. To go to Yonah Posvad, the head of the Zionists of our town, was impossible because he sold out to our foes during the elections and had become our enemy.

On the way, I ran into one of my dear friends by the name of Hofmann. Mr. Hofmann, the grandson of Kraindel Tscharney, the abandoned wife, was a partner in a certain bank in Szybusz and was free most of the day for leisurely conversation. In his youth he had loved the poetic rhythms of classical Hebrew, and this brought us closer together. Even though we disagreed on certain matters, like Zionism, which he would denigrate, since his brother-in-law, Mr. Levi Cohen, was a Zionist and from that he concluded that Zionism cannot be terribly important. Mr. Hofmann said, "The Messiah has not yet arrived, so why are you running so hard?" I said to him, "The Messiah has not come but his travails are already here." I immediately told him the whole saga of Alexander. Mr. Hofmann said, "We first need to check if he hasn't already been released in the meantime. Let's go and send a telegram to my brother-in-law Levi Cohen in Pishevits to look into the matter."

Along the way were joined by Mr. Itzhak Mundschpiel, the father of Vovi Mundschpiel, who said to Mr. Hofmann, "I'm on my way to see *your* wife, but since my wife isn't in town where are *you* off to?" Mr. Hofmann said to me, "Tell him the whole business." Mr. Mundschpiel said, "I knew from the start that I had the right to join up with you, because there's no way to keep a secret between two people."

Mr. Hofmann said to him, "I heard you went to visit your wife in Vienna. Pray tell whether you think she is considering coming back to you." He said to him, "Why would she come back? She has a job, she earns money. Young men court her as if she is the only woman in the world and sometimes they invite her to go horseback riding, and she has no shortage of libraries for romance novels, so why come back?" Mr. Hofmann said, "Hanukkah candles we light on the windowsill, but a good-looking woman we hide in the corner of the house." Mundschpiel smiled and said, "What will they do to her? After all, she's a married woman." And as he was speaking Mundschpiel took out a toy gun and said, "Look, I brought this thing as a present for your son Volvoly for *Lag BaOmer*. Now the animals will have to fear for their lives."

Itzhak Mundschpiel was from among the jokesters of Szybusz, but was not hated like the rest of the jokesters who derived pleasure from making fun of others. He had another way, which was to exaggerate everything. After he was widowed from his first wife, he landed up in Lemberg and there he used to come and go from the house of one householder who had a pretty daughter. Itzhak would sit with her and delight her with all sorts of crazy stories. Because of this she fell in love with him and wanted to marry him. He said to her, "Dear Miss, whatever has possessed you to set your eyes on an old widower like me who has an empty house and a money bag full of holes?" The lass was convinced that he was exaggerating and he became even more endeared to her. After she became his wife and came with him to Szybusz she began to get bored. One day she said to him, "Isaac, get me a horse to ride on." He responded, "A horse needs a stable." She said, "So then build us a stable." He said, "For a stable you need room." She said to him, "So then, get a lot." He answered, "To buy a lot requires money." She said to him, "If so, get some money." He said to her, "From where am I supposed to get money?" It didn't take long before she realized that he hadn't exaggerated and there was no more bread in the house. She sold some of her dresses and bought herself a ticket to Vienna with the proceeds and there she found employment at a bank, in keeping with her social status. At this bank, Itzhak Mundschpiel used to say, a person would come in to borrow money for a quarter of a year, and by the time he'd walk out of the building it was time for him to pay up his obligation. There was a special bureau there called the Stamp Bureau, where you would go to affix stamps to your letters. And a certain matron would stand there, her tongue sticking out the whole day long, and two Gentiles stood on either side of her, one to the right and one to the left, pouring water on her tongue so that it would remain very moist, and a dozen clerks ran to and fro wetting the stamps on her tongue. And there was that time that they forgot to dot the letter *i* for a whole year and saved millions on ink.

Upon arriving at the post office, we found the telegram room full of people with telegrams in their hands standing at the partially open window of Mr. Dovidzeni, who was in charge of telegrams, but he was paying them no mind. We waited more than a quarter of an hour. Itzhak Mundschpiel stood with us in line, entertaining himself with the revolver that he had brought as a gift for Volvoly. He was extolling the virtues of the bank where his wife worked, where a dedicated railroad had been installed connecting the bank with the telegram office, and not a moment passes that a special train doesn't leave the bank for the telegram office, laden with telegrams.

Out of fatigue Mr. Hofmann shuffled from foot to foot. We'd been standing there over a half-hour and the clerk still had not turned to his customers. Even if he had fallen asleep, it was already time for him to have awoken. Hofmann squeezed himself in and peered through the window. "What's that in his hand?" asked Hofmann amazed. Mundschpiel smiled and said, "You really didn't see?" Mr. Hofmann looked and said, "Unbelievable! How vulgar, and in front of all the women!" Mundschpiel pulled the trigger of the revolver. Suddenly the sound of a shot reverberated throughout the building. Mr. Dovidzeni dropped his pisspot in a panic. The men and women stood there dumbfounded. Dovidzeni paled in horror and stood frozen like a statue. The resonance of the shattering porcelain resembled wild laughter. Hofmann grabbed Mundschpiel angrily and shouted, "Come!" Mundschpiel laughed and said, "You're rushing as if the waters of the Strypa were on fire, heaven forbid."

Dovidzeni recovered and screamed, "Who is the one who dared do this!?" Itzhak Mundschpiel took a slight bow and said, "The Socialists, great and enlightened lord. Today is May first, their holiday." Dovidzeni screamed and yelled, "I'm going to send an urgent telegram to Lemberg, son of a bitch! Tomorrow the town will be teeming with regiments, son of a bitch! I'll assail you with an entire battalion, son of a bitch!"

After Dovidzeni's anger had abated, Hofmann gave him the telegram and said to me, "Until now there hasn't been a greater lobbyist than my brother-in-law, but now that he voted for Davidsohn one has to wonder if he might be harmful to our cause. Go instead to Bürgermeister Zanvil, and with just one word he'll free your Russian." Mr. Hofmann continued and said, "When I think about Zanvil, it saddens me. The curse of a small town hangs over him. What greatness he could have attained for himself in a large town. Just think of it, a man who was incarcerated in jail, not only do they set him free but they then heap greatness upon his greatness. How did this happen? They needed to organize elections for the legislature and the provincial officer sent a telegram to the electoral commissioner saying that without Sebastian Montag (Zanvil had been Montag's prior name) it would be impossible. They immediately removed Zanvil from prison and restored his honor. It's not for nothing that the Socialists holler that the whole country is driven by the word of Zanvil Montag. And not only is he very powerful in politics but in every single thing. I'd be shocked if there is anyone in this generation who knows the will of the masses the way he does. Things that should be embarrassing infuse him with glory. On those occasions when he leaves the bar, crooning either religious or bawdy melodies to his delight, Zanvil latches on to a passing Jew and asks him, 'When does the Jewish new month fall?' Immediately the Jew is impressed and says, 'A man whose place is among the greats of Poland, and yet he still doesn't neglect Judaism.' And not just with Jews does he know how to hold his own but also with the Polish nobility. One when time a certain nobleman got up in the city council hall to oppose him, what did Zanvil do? He dipped his finger in saliva and touched the neck of the officer as if he'd found a flea there and threw it to the ground and crushed it with his foot. The officer recognized the favor right away, thanked him and didn't open his mouth against him the entire night. In short, go to Zanvil and make an effort with him and I'm certain that he'll get the Russian out of prison. And what do you have to say about the duel? Szybusz has gotten to be a real city."

Chapter Sixteen

The Sword and the Book

Great was the happiness of Volvoly, who was thrilled with the revolver that Mr. Itzhak Mundschpiel had given him. The little devil tied his weapon around his hip and walked around like a warrior, terrifying the entire household with shots and singing:

> *I am Teschil, I'm police cop*
> *I can slap and I can clop*
> *I shoot my gun: "Bang! Bang!"*
> *I rule the entire gang*
> *I shoot my gun: "Pi poi!"*
> *The Jews all holler: "Oy!"*

Itzhak Mundschpiel patted Volvoly lovingly on his shoulder and said, "A hero." Mrs. Hofmann took her son in both her arms and kissed him loudly on the lips. Mr. Hofmann shook his head and said, "New ideals. Teschil, the policeman... What the grownups ponder in back rooms, little children proclaim from mountain tops. Each generation has its ideals. I'm reminded of the man who hit his son who had become lax about Torah and said to him, 'If you don't study, you will end up like that.' And the *that* was a general. As Hofmann was speaking a scream was heard in the room. Volvoly was frightening his little sister with his weapon. Mrs. Hofmann took the little one in her arms and cajoled her with pleasant things. She said to her, "If you stop crying Uncle Hemdat will tell you a sweet little story like 'Rabbi Gadiel the Infant' or 'The Tale of the Woodchopper' or 'The Legend of the Messiah'." But Cornelia took particular pleasure in her crying and wouldn't stop. Her father castigated her and said, "Hush, you Kraindel Tscharney, you! Are you the only one suffering here?" Cornelia quieted down somewhat, then resumed her crying. I stood and took her in my arms and propped her up on my knee and started to tell her story after story until her mind was at rest and she took my arm and moved it back and forth like a mother rocking her child, singing a Hebrew lullaby.

Hofmann looked at his little daughter and his face lit up. Mrs. Hofmann said, "You see, Sir. My husband, may he live a long life, is just like his grandmother Kraindel Tscharney, may she rest in peace. Even though he screams and hollers and chastises, he has a good heart. Not only that, but if he curses and swears he immediately regrets it. A family flaw." Mr. Hofmann waved off her praises of him and pointed to his little son and said, "You see this boy? This boy, it's as if he isn't from our family. At first, I would have said that he resembled Menashe Chaim, the first husband of my grandmother Kraindel Tscharney, rest in peace, because I noticed that he causes pain to others." Mr. Hofmann had not had a chance to finish his thought, when Mrs. Hofmann raised her hand towards him in alarm and said, "Stop tempting fate!" and, while speaking, she spit three times. Mr. Hofmann said, "Menashe Chaim was a decent man, except he was born under a bad sign."

The servant set the table and brought bread and butter and cream and eggs and radishes and green onions and milk and coffee. Mrs. Hofmann invited me to have supper with them, but out of respect for my father's house, lest they think that there was not enough food back at home, I declined and took leave for my house.

Chapter Seventeen

Praise For the Bürgermeister in His Absence

Our Bürgermeister didn't like me and it could be he even hated me, because of the evil ones who slandered me to him. What happened was like this: When the rumor of the Kishinev pogroms reached Szybusz, the entire town was inspired to organize a large memorial service at the synagogue and raise money for the orphans. In time, a letter from Szybusz was published in a certain newspaper and this is more or less what it said: *In our town they also eulogized the slain of the pogrom, etc., etc. The rabbinical judge prayed for the well being of the monarchy, and when he concluded the students rose up and sang the Jewish national anthem, "Our hope is not yet lost...," etc., etc.* Now, the report seemed to be critiquing the head of the rabbinical court for failing to eulogize correctly, and the aristocracy for not showing up because the eulogy was not given in Polish, and the community for not raising funds for the benefit of the victims of the pogroms, and the Jewish Bürgermeister for not attending the service. That letter caused a great ruckus in our town. For Szybusz, although it clings to tradition, knows the value of a newspaper and the value of the printed word. Not too many days had passed before a second letter from Szybusz was published, even harsher than the first which began,

"By virtue of Clause 19 of the laws of publishing I hereby demand that space be allotted for the following lines:"

a) The rabbinical judge was forced to speak about the well being of the monarchy, inasmuch as he had been preoccupied by a dispute between the ritual slaughterers and hadn't had time to prepare a new speech, and so he used an already prepared speech that he had delivered on the Emperor's birthday.

b) Not because the eulogy hadn't been in Polish did the aristocracy fail to show up for the memorial, but rather that same day they had been busy with a ball, and even angels can't perform two missions simultaneously, let alone mortals.

c) Money for the pogrom victims couldn't possibly have been raised, because pockets had already been emptied the day before when the mayor of the city collected monies for a ball that his wife was making.

d) From reading the newspaper's previous editorial, it was evident that the writer was not at all a member of the community and didn't know things that even a babe in the woods would know – that the Bürgermeister had not come to the memorial as he had been incarcerated in prison for using counterfeit playing cards, and so on.

That was roughly the language of the letter that was printed based on Clause 19 of the laws of publishing and in which the people of Szybusz saw a hidden agenda to bring back to mind the disgrace of the Bürgermeister. And they whispered to the Bürgermeister that I was the one who'd written the letter, and because of this the Bürgermeister had developed a dislike for me.

To be honest, with the approaching elections he began to get close to me, but this closeness wasn't rooted in affection but rather in politics. In those days, there was not a man in Szybusz whose shoulder the Bürgermeister would not pat affectionately. His enemies became his close friends. But throughout the election period I did not say anything negative about him, like all my other friends, being certain that his hostility against me had dissipated.

Chapter Eighteen
For the Land and For Its Sustenance

I found myself a leniency to get a haircut during the Days of the Omer, when pious Jews generally don't shave or cut their hair, and I donned my Sabbath clothes and went up to see the Bürgermeister. The Bürgermeister received me warmly and inquired about my well-being and that of my grandfather, heaping great praise on my grandfather. My grandfather had been a community leader for forty years but ultimately left those responsibilities behind to dedicate himself fulltime to Talmud study. The Bürgermeister ventured, "We had ourselves one smart counselor in this town and he went and relinquished his position to fools." I said to the Bürgermeister, "My grandfather has given up all other pleasures, save the study of Talmud." After that I relayed to the Bürgermeister the matter of Alexander. The Bürgermeister responded and said, "I need only give the provincial officer one hint and he will at once release your Nikolai from prison. The provincial officer does everything I say, because if not for me his friend wouldn't have been elected to the legislature. Don't I always say that we must live in peace with the government? And so screamed the prophet Jeremiah, 'Seek the welfare of the city, for in its peace you shall have peace.' As our sages said, 'Honor the physician before thou hast need of him,' and if the Poles don't always act properly towards the Jews, well a worm can be found even in a sweet apple." I said to the Bürgermeister, "The truth is that the worm is evidence that the apple is sweet, but woe to the apple that the worm consumes in its entirety." However, the Bürgermeister had no need to hear this and he continued and said, "You think I'm not a Zionist, but I am, I am the consummate Zionist, not like those whippersnappers who can't read a single Hebrew letter. You're the one about whom they say, 'He's a master of the holy tongue,' so can you really stomach listening to their lectures? They have the tone of a whining, old proselyte. I'm not claiming to be free from all sin and transgression, even God is not clear of all sin as the adage goes, for after all He is the one who created the world. You think that it's easy being the leader of the town? On account of every plague – *with which may the community never be visited!* – they come to me sounding the alarm. When the Hasids in Pishevits break the rabbi's windows and get thrown in jail, to whom do they come to get released? To me! Rabbi Meir of Premishlan used to say, 'One time I passed the gates of hell. I glanced in and saw that one of the angels of destruction was standing before the oven, an iron skewer in his hand, and a stout, rotund rabbi was affixed to the top of the skewer, being roasted in the fire. And every now and then the angel would take a scrawny Hasid, thin as a matchstick, and toss him into the flames to stoke the fire.' You know what, Sir, that's as it should be. Roast the rabbis and throw the Hasids into the blaze and I guarantee you there will be peace for the Jews. Have you ever seen a Jew admiring the modern leaders? You know why not? Because he doesn't know their language and they don't know his. About them it is admonished, 'I will bring a nation upon you from afar, a nation whose language thou knowest not.' Come let me show you some things I wrote in my youth in *HaMagid* under a pen name, about standing up for noble causes like when my grandfather, may he rest in peace, donated a handsome sum for the benefit of the synagogue. But since you're obviously so fond of the commandment of redeeming captives, let's not miss the opportunity."

The Bürgermeister took me by the arm and we went out to the street. We hadn't been walking more than two or three minutes when he stopped and said, "Seeing as we're right near Oberschenkil's tavern, let's go in. Wine is as good for an old man as milk is for a baby."

The Bürgermeister asked Oberschenkil, "Anything to taste? Anything to taste? The clock is ticking. The clock is ticking. We have important business. Give us whatever you've got, a bit of anything, just to fulfill the obligation of taking a taste. I have already had my morning meal. From the time I reached the age of reason, I've always been conscientious about breakfast. Didn't our sages say, 'sixty men cannot overtake one who has early meals in the morning'?"

The proprietor began to list the dishes he had available and said, "We have carp cooked in honey and roasted goose, and truffles and mushrooms coated in egg." The Bürgermeister shouted, "Truffles and mushrooms? Truffles and mushrooms?! Are we in the mournful first nine days of Av?! Bring what you'll bring and just hurry up. Fish first. What do we drink before? Kümmel schnapps? And after the fish, bring the goose. Is it stuffed with apples?" Oberschenkil said, "Regretfully, the goose is not stuffed with apples, but we have instead roasted pigeons stuffed with apples and cinnamon." The Bürgermeister said, "Pray tell, who is it who can afford to order himself such a large feast? For myself, I am satisfied with just bread and butter. Were it not for the fact that I have to interact with the Gentiles, I would make do with bread and garlic, except that then they would say that Jews reek. Do you think they are as pure as angels? Baron Pitshinski bathes daily in spirit of turpentine but even so no one can stand his odor."

When Oberschenkil brought out a platter of fish the Bürgermeister asked him, "So what do we drink after it?" Oberschenkil answered, "Cherry and plum and egg yolk and peach wines, white wine and honey wine, sherry and cinnamon, cognac and arak." Said the Bürgermeister, "I like simple brandy, brandy made from grain, not the kind from Szybusz, but so as not to embarrass you I'll let you also serve the other beverages. I beseech you to remove the small glass from here. It's nothing but a waste of time to pour and then pour again, as if there's nothing in the world but drinking. Bring a glass like one that's used for drinking tea, or a mug that's used for beer."

The sounds of clinking coins and the shuffling of cards were heard from the other room. Sebastian asked the proprietor, "Who's in there?" The proprietor whispered to him. Sebastian said, "Don't tell them I'm here. What are they playing?" The proprietor whispered to him. Suddenly, the Bürgermeister's eyes lit up and he was about to go and join them. At the same moment, Miss Oberschenkil came in. Her face was as inflamed as a baker's oven during a year of plenty and she was holding Przybyszewski's *The Snow* under her arm. When she saw the Bürgermeister she nodded her head towards him. The Bürgermeister greeted her and said, "How are you, my girl?" She answered him and said, "Hello, Mr. Bürgermeister, Sir." The Bürgermeister asked, "And how is your fiancé? If I'm not mistaken Gold is his name?" Miss Oberschenkil said, "Zilber." The Bürgermeister said, "It's not the name that's of the essence." She greeted me and said in surprise, "Even your honor is here?" I bowed my head so she wouldn't see my face and returned her greeting. After Miss Oberschenkil left the room the Bürgermeister said, "My good boy, your face is so red we could fry fish on it! Indeed, it would be worth waiting even seven years for a girl like that."

The Bürgermeister continued, "The truth is I'm not fond of petite women. A small woman doesn't know love and when she does love, she does so only tenuously. She lacks the kind of passion possessed by real women, so it is easy to win her heart. But the big women, that is to say the tall ones, most of them are devoted to their husbands. I'm not saying all, but certainly most of them. And when it comes to transgressions, a tall one who has given herself over to transgression, there is in her surrender a kind of incomprehensible suffering and delight. It feels as though I'm both her lover and her husband all rolled into one, and not only that but the awareness of sin, in other words she knows that she's committing a sin, and her being poised on the threshold of hell lends the union an animal force. And I'll also tell you this, a tall one who has seduced another can't cope with her transgression and she torments herself and doesn't stop clamoring until she has made her husband a party to her sorrow and he is saddened and weeps along with her, not because she has hurt him but rather he is crying over her broken heart. I know there are men whose wives have affairs and who make like they don't even know. These miserable creatures just want to live a seemingly peaceful and honorable life and they greet their wives' paramours warmly and fatten them up with their food. And I'll tell you something else. Most of those paramours are lowlifes who have neither courage nor strength, and what is more they are driven by primal instincts, eager for married women because they don't know the secret of purity and because they intend to sully that purity that people make a mockery of. I once had a small-time clerk in my department, the type who writes poetry and articles. He went and seduced a pregnant woman whose belly was already out to here. From the time I reached the age of reason, I've looked at a pregnant woman as though the righteous redeemer himself is hidden within her." The Bürgermeister's lips were dry from so much talking and he stood and poured himself a glass of the honey wine to moisten them. Oberschenkil brought out the goose and the pigeons. The Bürgermeister nodded his head with fondness for the roasted fowl. After eating and drinking he arose and leaning on me said, "We really should go and compliment Mrs. Oberschenkil in person. Come, let's go to the kitchen."

We couldn't make out the form of a single person in the kitchen due to the haze from all the cooking. When we began peering through the mist, we saw Mrs. Oberschenkil standing at the stove. The Bürgermeister sought to compliment her in person until he espied a plump hen in the midst of being roasted, whereupon he lost his powers of speech. At that moment, the proprietress inserted her finger into the hen to check and see if its meat was tender enough and she turned it and sprinkled it with some fine flour mixed with oil and with white wine and lemon juice and then sprinkled it with salt and pepper, took it from the fire and adorned it with a glaze of egg yolk. When he had regained his powers of speech, the Bürgermeister asked the proprietress, "For whom is this hen?" The proprietress answered humbly, "Would that His Highness honor us and taste my handiwork?"

I gathered up my courage and I said, "My lord Bürgermeister, I'm afraid that meanwhile the provincial officer might go to bed." The Bürgermeister placed his hand on my shoulder and said, "Set your mind at ease, dear friend, as long as the provincial officer isn't here it's certain he's not asleep. I'm sure we'll find him playing cards at Chazermeyrinski's or at Schweintochinski's bar or at Calbinski's store or at Mrs. Bushavecherpinski. But why are you not trying all this good food?"

Teschil the police deputy arrived with a bundle of booklets in his hand. Oberschenkil brought a pen and ink and the Bürgermeister signed them. And as he was doing it he said to me, "You see that I don't need spectacles." After signing his name he asked, "That's it?" The police lieutenant bowed to him and said, "That's it, my lord Bürgermeister." Even so, Teschil didn't budge an inch. Sebastian looked at him in surprise. Teschil bowed again and said, "Fosvad says that the lord Bürgermeister gave him permission to charge every monger in the marketplace for the right to her stall." Sebastian peered at Teschil and said, "Do I not have the right to permit it, Mister?" Teschil cowered and said, "Sir, yes sir, my lord Bürgermeister, of course, of course it's your right my lord Bürgermeister, who would deny it, my lord Bürgermeister?" Sebastian said, "If so, then what have you come to tell me, dear sir?" Teschil responded, "When Fosvod came to collect the money one woman got up and threw a stool at his head." Sebastian clapped his hands and said, "Nicely done, valiant daughter!" Suddenly, the Bürgermeister's expression changed and he said angrily, "When he was a Zionist he used to sit and wait for a license, but from me he looks for immediate payback."

The hen was brought out to the table with a bowl full of rice and a lovely garland of Turkish pepper surrounding the rice. Sebastian took out his spectacles and cleaned them diligently and said, "Come and let us see what we'll do to that hen," and he gazed upon it with satisfaction and pleasure.

Oberschenkil asked the Bürgermeister, "What shall I bring my lord Bürgermeister for his dessert?" "Nothing at all, nothing at all," said the Bürgermeister. "Other tavern masters also must pay taxes. They too have to make a living. We must go immediately to Chazermeyrinski's, but in any event you can bring out two or three kinds ofnuts and a bottle of white wine, or even better some shelled almonds and red wine. Shelled almonds and red wine are pretty to look at."

The Bürgermeister put two nuts into his fist to crack them and said, "Rabbi Moshe Chaim, that 'enlightened' one is naturally curious by nature, and claims that everything is dependent on the air. The air is the working force. It's not the hand that breaks the nut open, but rather the air that does it. How is that? Air goes in and pushes the nut and immediately it cracks open. Moshe Chaim himself couldn't crack even a small nut in his hands, and when they mocked him and said, 'Where's your know-how, Moshe Chaim?' what did he answer? 'That's what I told you, it's the air, it's all in the power of the air.' Apparently, insufficient air had gotten in."

Sebastian took his watch out of his pocket, looked at it and said, "If we don't hurry, we'll find Chazermeyrinski's shop closed. You see, my dear friend, it's a good thing that the Socialists didn't win and they don't lock up the establishments at eight o'clock. Oberschenkil, bring the bill." And in the midst of speaking he got up, took out a toothpick, picked his teeth with it and said, "You don't have to rush so much. In any case, I have no money on me." Oberschenkil bowed to him and said, "Never mind, my lord Bürgermeister," and gestured with his finger through the window towards the new bar and said, "He's still serving over there." The Bürgermeister stored the toothpick in his pocket and said, "Perhaps you'd like me to go have dinner over there?" Oberschenkil's face turned green. The Bürgermeister donned his hat and said, "Tomorrow Teschil will come and shut down his restaurant." Oberschenkil jumped for joy and said, "My lord Bürgermeister, we can say that imported spirits were found at his place or that..." The Bürgermeister interrupted him and said, "No need for justifications, no need for justifications. I prefer a simple story without interpretation. Come let's go to Chazermeyrinski. To save a life. What's the Russian's name?" Before we even got to Chazermeyrinski's store we found out that the provincial officer had gone elsewhere. The Bürgermeister called for a ride. The coachman came with his carriage. The Bürgermeister ascended and said to me, "Come tomorrow or better yet the day after tomorrow, in case I'm tired tomorrow and you will have troubled yourself needlessly. A clever chap that Goethe. At times he would spend the entire day in bed, even when he was not sick."

Chapter Nineteen
On That Night Hath Fled the Sleep

After the toils of the day I didn't find rest that night either. Both because of lack of space in father's house, and so that my grandfather would not sleep alone in the room, I used to sleep in his room on my late grandmother's bed, may she rest in peace.

Tscharney Rivka, the maid, opened the door for me. She was still awake and about to wash the last bowl from supper. It was quiet in the house, the windows were shut and the drapes were drawn. The large clock glistened from the wall as it ticked away. Suddenly an elf emerged from the clock with a small hammer in its hand and struck ten times. It was already ten o'clock and my grandfather was already lying in bed. Fortunately he wouldn't see that I'd gotten a haircut during the Omer period. Even though I had found a leniency to get a haircut I feared that he would be strict with me. I took off my clothing and entered the bed chamber. My grandfather lay on his bed, his long pipe in his mouth and his lips murmured in his sleep, "*Pah, pah, pah.*" I got into my bed and recited the *Shema Yisrael* prayer but my body found no rest. My head was spinning and my eyes burned like they had been sprinkled with salt and I felt like jumping out of my skin. And the pillow, because it sensed that I had gotten a haircut and my hair was not soft, began to push against my head and my head pushed back, and between the pillow and the head I was deprived of my rest.

A heavy sigh escaped from my grandfather's heart. I shuddered and buried my head in the pillow, trying to ignore that sigh, but when he sighed again I could no longer ignore it. This old man, who had reached the age of eighty years and whom I'd never heard sigh in all the time I had known him – even on the Ninth of Av – was now moaning. I raised myself a bit and said, "Grandfather, are you not asleep?" My grandfather, as though he had been expecting this question, raised himself up, covered his pipe with his thumb and shook up the embers, wiped off his hands and said, "How can I sleep when God has withdrawn his loving kindness from you and fails to safeguard you from going down the wrong path? *Oy*, Hemdat, Hemdat, the torments of Job are upon me, only the Holy One has not found me as upright as Job so as to merit a blessed ending." My grandfather lit the candle and rekindled the flame in his pipe and smoked it. The small volume of Talmud that he always kept by his bedside was not open, as he'd already intended to go to sleep but sleep had fled from him. The flickering of candlelight on his white beard reminded me of winter nights when I used to go to study Torah, lantern in hand. My grandfather took a few puffs and said, "I had hoped to live in serenity with Torah and service to God. I had said to myself, 'May my aching body be bound up in the warmth of the oven at the morning watch as I'm hunched over a page of Gemara, and may I derive pleasure from my offspring.' Szybusz is still sitting without a rabbi and I had been expecting to see you assume the rabbinical post. Pray tell me, what it is you find in those books that you squander your time on? I was curious and took a peek at those Hasidic tales. At first I thought that they were essentially a joke, but I finally realized that those fools seriously thought they were getting at the truth, as it were. I beseech you to tell me, what will this deceit do for you? I threw them under the bed. Perhaps you regret your prior path, tell Tscharney Rivka to remove them. You've now reached the age to take a wife and what will we say to the in-laws? Hemdat buried his head in nonsense?"

And here my grandfather sighed yet a third time and said, "I'll be doing myself an injustice if I complain that I was unsuccessful in my old age. But how is it possible for my soul to depart this world in peace when you are losing both this world and the next all at once. *Ach*, this is an age of upheaval. In the past we would learn in the study house to the light of a dim wick, six or seven students to one worn and tattered book and even so there was no darkness in our world. If only I could feel at the hour of my demise a small fraction of the sweetness that I felt in my youth. And now, thank God, all the study houses are filled with fine books, all of them with legible print, and you have removed yourself from the Torah. Here I am a man of eighty years and I rise up and go to bed every day, thank God, immersed in Torah and Jewish law, and my youngster of a grandson wastes his days and nights on books of nonsense. Is this what the Torah meant when it said, 'You shall meditate upon it day and night?' Please tell me, what pleasure do you derive from them?"

Short was the night and I had hardly slept at all, yet even so the dream master found time to frighten me with strange dreams. For example, the daughter of Shalmaneser danced before me naked. She was sloe-eyed, her pupils prancing within her almond-like eyes, redder than wine. Facing her stood Rabbi Joseph Della Reina and he appeared to me in the likeness of Sebastian Montag, the Bürgermeister, and he was warning her not to vote for Dr. Davidsohn, for if she voted for Dr. Davidsohn she would be ousted from the "Ruth Sisterhood." And in mid-speech he began to dance before her and sing his bawdy song. Here's how it goes:

When I was just a miss
My charm set hearts aflutter
I'd give a hug and kiss
To get a chunk of butter.

As he was dancing, Lilith appeared, grasped Alexander and led him to the mountains of darkness. And there was one more person there, I don't remember who it was, perhaps Pope Joan, who gesticulated wildly yelling, "So is it proper and so is it fitting for you, sinner of Israel."

Chapter Twenty
A Nameless Chapter

There was no telegram from Pishevits. Hofmann was angry and said, "My brother-in-law, because he is so occupied with the salvation of all of Jewry, hasn't the time to rescue even one Jewish soul. Well, I'll send him a telegram that he'll remember even on his death bed!" On our way to the post office we saw bands and bands of people standing in the marketplace shouting, "So is it proper and so is it fitting for you, people of Szybusz." And their fellow townsmen shouting back at them, "And aren't you yourselves also from Szybusz? If so, why are you staying silent?" They responded, "Is that so? We are staying silent? Indeed, we are standing here and shouting." They answered back, "Woe to that sort of shouting. We are also shouting like that and what good comes from all these shouts? If only there were unity amongst the Jews, we could do great things." Itzhak Mundschpiel laughed and said, "With unity it's possible to get a quorum of ten for public worship. As there has not been one day without shouting since the time of the elections, I haven't paid any attention to the shouting. I thought the Bürgermeister had sent a policeman to torment a beggar or that that he had closed down the new tavern."

Mr. Hofmann asked Itzhak Mundschpiel, "What is all the shouting about?" Mundschpiel answered, "Zanvil Montag ordered that Kiddush and Havdalah be brought to Mr. Dovidzeni." Said Mr. Hofmann, "Mundschpiel, quit your joking around and tell us why Szybusz is shouting so much." Mundschpiel replied, "Because of Mr. Dovidzeni, the telegram clerk, who has betrayed his duty. Already the merchants had been astounded and complaining bitterly that some of their telegrams remained unanswered. But remember that foreigner who came here from Germany? He sent a telegram from Szybusz, and when it wasn't answered he conducted investigations and inquiries until it was discovered that Dovidzeni has been keeping the telegram fees for himself and not sending the telegrams. In truth, the deficit hadn't been noticed, inasmuch as Dovidzeni is old and works only infrequently, the rest of the time his assistants fill in, and so he didn't have enough time to steal too much. During a two week period, six kroner went missing. No claims are being made for the other monies that he had hidden earlier. Even though Mr. Dovidzeni was the honored president of the Polish sports club, they removed him from his high post, for his friends were embarrassed that for the sake of six kroner he had embezzled and stolen. The Jewish merchants collected the six missing kroner amongst themselves and gave them to the postmaster to reconcile the accounts." I said to Hofmann, "Sir, it is for naught that you suspected your brother in law of not answering your telegram." Hofmann said, "Take this as a general principal: if you slap a Jew in the face and he doesn't deserve it today, he'll surely deserve it by tomorrow."

Chapter Twenty-One

Measure for Measure, *or*
Fashion Versus Fashion

A metal-work merchant came to town and hawked his wares in the markets and the roads calling out, "Who wants metal-work? Who wants metal-work?"

> *Some traps for your mice?*
> *A strainer or a sieve?*
> *My birdcages are nice*
> *With rare mesh weave.*
>
> *Metal hooks of every kind*
> *Some curved and some plain*
> *Holes and spaces you'll find*
> *All things in that vein.*
>
> *Grab one for your house*
> *Dear ladies, dear gents*
> *They'll kill each and every mouse*
> *That's lurking in your vents.*

All the people in the road literally were tugging on his sleeve and buying mousetraps.

One woman said to her friend, "It's an upside-down world we live in. The mice are bigger than the cats. I have cats in the house and even so the mice ate my new dress. I hadn't worn it yet, hadn't even touched it and along came a mouse." And her friend answered and said, "You think my mice are any better than yours? If only I could be rid of them all in one day. You're crying about your clothing and I about my sick husband." Her friend said to her, "Since when is your husband sick?" She said to her, "Since when? Since this past Sabbath eve." She said to her, "And what caused your husband to be sick?" She said to her, "What caused him to be sick? On the eve of the Sabbath he forgot to check our marriage contract and when he lay down to go to sleep he discovered that the mice had chewed it up. He stood and jumped out of bed and ran off naked and barefoot and caught a chill."

The peddler stood in the upper marketplace, hawking his wares and singing:

> *In one town in our nation*
> *At a most auspicious hour*
> *In the holy congregation*
> *A new leader came to power.*
>
> *Right away did his wife make*
> *A kugel fat and scrumptious*
> *A stove-sized one she baked*
> *With raisins in abundance.*
>
> *For the Sabbath after prayers*
> *A celebration had been planned*
> *But listen carefully while I share*
> *What then happened to that man.*
>
> *Mice, their names be blotted out*
> *Smelled the kugel's fine aroma*

And congregated thereabout
Not leaving one iota.

The food of noble royalty
Is a kugel sweet and fat
May God find me as worthy
And fill my needs like that.

A moral and a warning bell
Get a snare for your abode
To avoid this fate as well
And now our story's told.

Even my grandfather purchased a mousetrap. The books he had thrown under the bed had been attacked by mice. All of Szybusz was amazed and asked, "What prompted Rabbi Yakir to follow the latest fad? After all, he despises all contemporary fashions." And as it so happens when my grandmother, may she rest in peace, once brought home a new silver dish, my grandfather had indeed thrown it out saying, "I despise falsehood and pride." My grandfather opened his tobacco pouch, smiled and said, "Fashion versus fashion, just like measure for measure. Against mice that totally destroyed new-fangled books that are 'in fashion' there is no choice but to use an instrument of destruction that is also in fashion. Today they eat nonsensical books and tomorrow they will devour my slippers." Then my grandfather said to me, "The Holy One Blessed Be He gave mice the wisdom to discern between good and evil. It so happens that I bought myself a copy of *The Paths of the World*, by Abraham Menahem Mendel Mohr and the bookbinder, boor that he was, who would bind together a page of the Haggadah with a page of Lamentations, bound together Mendel Mohr's book with *The Gate of Reward* by Nachmanides. One time I was in Lemberg and found Mendel Mohr standing in the railway station ripping into a loaf of bread without performing the ritual hand washing, and it was very difficult for me to behold. When I returned home I put away his book, because to destroy it completely was impossible because of its neighbor Nachmanides, may he rest in peace. And so I stored it up in my attic. Eventually I went up there and when I held the book in my hands I saw that the mice had not left even one full page of Mohr intact, yet they hadn't touched the *The Gate of Reward* at all." My grandfather took the mousetrap, put it in my hands and said, "Give this to Tscharney Rivka but don't tell her which books the mice ate – the very ones that she had been foolishly kissing."

Chapter Twenty-Two
Peace Upon Israel

As Rabbi Binyamin so aptly put it, "What is not accomplished by way of common sense, will be accomplished by the lack thereof." On the very night that Gold had cried, "Encore!" Miss Oberschenkil had jilted him and given her heart to Zilber, who had zealously protected the honor of a woman affronted and risked his life so chivalrously. And she had written him a long letter, filled with praise. And not only in writing had she praised him but also in person, those times that they had gone strolling among the graves of the Gentiles in the darkness of night. Zilber had known then that even if all the students of Szybusz came to court her, she would never withdraw her affections from him. Every time that Zilber would return happy and tired from Steffi Oberschenkil, he would go to Mrs. Zilberman and relay the secrets of his heart. I don't know what Zilber's intent was, to boast of his conquests as young men are wont to do or to arouse jealousy in the heart of Mrs. Zilberman, because jealousy leads to love. In any event, Mrs. Zilberman, that upright woman, did not find fault with the stories of conquest. And when he would praise Miss Oberschenkil, Mrs. Zilberman would agree with every single thing that Zilber said. When that arrogant one saw that this was the case, he sensed that she was smitten with him. Immediately his heart coarsened towards her and he began to say things to her that he never would have dared say before. And the jokesters of Szybusz were already deriving material from the names Zilber and Zilberman. "Who knows," they said, "who here is the real man?"

Doctor Zilberman was modest and he didn't like people talking about him, even in praise. He did not like the idea that a duel had come about on account of his wife, and already Gold's mother had come to him crying and saying, "One of the lambs will be slain." Doctor Zilberman recalled the words of that woman who had said to him, "Get on there, you fool. Get on!" while gesturing to him to get onto the carriage and go with his aunt to Lemberg. Zilberman knew that Zilber would never go to war. Close to the event he would back away. He had never even seen weapons in his life. All day long he'd be running from Steffi Oberschenkil to his wife and from his wife to Steffi Oberschenkil. Like a hero, like a victor. To hell with him. That day Zilberman entered his house, his heart full of rage. He hadn't yet had a chance to relax and compose himself when the maid came in and said, "The apothecary is standing in the hallway." "Show him in," said Mrs. Zilberman. In came Zilber, took her right hand, pulled up the edge of her sleeve and his bushy moustache crept along her arm like a mouse, giving her a long kiss. Greeting her husband he asked, "Am I disturbing?" And from the tone of his question it was obvious that he was certain that he wasn't disturbing anyone. Zilberman returned his greeting warmly and said, "Heaven forbid." Zilber took a seat next to Mrs. Zilberman. As soon as he was seated, Zilberman grabbed him and threw him out.

On that very day the duel was cancelled. Gold took upon himself to dedicate a page in honor of Zilber in the Golden Book and, for his part, Zilber gave up the defense of Mrs. Zilberman's honor for the sake of the Jewish National Fund. And these were the terms of the donation: Gold would have to donate a third of the funds himself, and as for the remainder he could either give it from his own funds or if he preferred to raise it from others he would be allowed to do so. The first ten kroner would have to be given up front and the remainder of the first third little by little, until he became a doctor, and if he married first he would give from the dowry. And already from the publicity in the newspaper of the initial contribution of ten kroner came another ten kroner from a certain so-and-so, and when they counted they saw that Dr. Zilberman had donated to the fund in the name of the apothecary Mr. Zilber, to appease him for having thrown him out of the house and thereby having diminished his esteem in the eyes of Mrs. Zilberman. Even I sent in eighteen pence in Zilber's name as he had not withheld his mercy from Gold, thus saving a Jewish life.

And it's already being discussed in town that in the near future Zilber will be able to decorate his home with his page from the Golden Book, for Miss Oberschenkil remembered Mr. Gold's earlier acts of kindness and gave him back her heart. And there are those who are saying that they'll be erecting the wedding canopy shortly and Gold will give a portion of the dowry to the national fund and complete the donation in honor of Zilber. Another two or three of these sorts of duels and Szybusz will be at the forefront of the donors to the Jewish National Fund. Now I can go to Pishevits without having to worry about something awful happening back here, heaven forbid.

Chapter Twenty-Three
With Words of Jewish Law

My father said to me, "When you get to Pishevits, go see the rabbi and tell him from me that the new Torah interpretation that he told me about in Chortkov is actually attributed to Rabbi Yaakov Schorr, and it had already been formulated even earlier by the sage Rabbi Zalman Margolis. I am sure that the rabbi from Pishevits will be happy to learn that he was in agreement with important learned scholars. Do you want to hear, my son, or perhaps you are preoccupied with your trip and cannot pay attention to words of Torah? However, our sages bestowed good advice upon us when they said, 'A person should only take leave of his fellow amidst a discussion of Jewish law.' And I am telling you that there is deep meaning in this because a man is distracted from the perils of the journey by words of Torah and is thus not so anxious. So listen."

My father then related the particular teaching found in the Jerusalem Talmud on which the Rabbi of Pishevits asked his purportedly insightful question. I wasn't clever enough to suggest my own solution and said to father, "Truly this is an important question that the Pishevits rabbi posed. What is the answer?"

My father said to me, "You see, my son, you ask why but you don't know how to resolve the problem, yet Rabbi Yankele Schorr at the age of fourteen could both pose difficult questions and provide answers, and here you are, praise God, a lad of eighteen years and you have to wait for others to come and render solutions. Are you familiar with Moshe Chaim? He used to say to his son Berish, 'Berish my son, when Franz Joseph was your age he was already an emperor, and you, my son, what are you?' But let's get back to the issue at hand. You ask why Rabbi Hiyya didn't go out and preach immediately. I remember when you used to ask harder questions than that within mere seconds. When I'm reminded of the new meaning you thought up regarding what Rabbi Samuel said, 'If they would bring me mushrooms, or a pigeon to Abba, would we not go on eating?' I derive so much pleasure and regret – pleasure that you came up with such an important new interpretation, and regret that you've separated yourself from the Torah. So do you wish to hear the solution?"

After father had lectured me about these things he said to me, "And what do you say about this solution, my son?" I said to him, "It sounds acceptable." He said to me, "The solution is a solution. However, the question is not a question." I said to him, "What do you mean the question is not a question?" He said, "I reviewed the entire Jerusalem Talmud and could not find any reference to this matter, and so it was for naught that all the sages deliberated to find a solution." I stood there, astonished, and thought to myself: "In the entire Jerusalem Talmud?" My father added, "When you see the Pishevits rabbi, you don't have to call him 'Rabbi,' as he bought himself the rabbinate with money, but act respectfully towards him for he is a Torah scholar and his ancestors were famous scholars. And now go in safety and peace and come back in safety and in peace. Make sure you didn't forget to take your *tefillin* with you."

Chapter Twenty-Four
In Praise of Our Modern Literature

Mr. Notkiss's remarks, while lamenting to me that his thoughts would always atrophy because he had no friends, were really puzzling. You should know that this was truly the case, because when I visited him in Pishevits and we sat on the porch of his father's house outside of town, eating strawberries with cream and sugar and looked at the setting sun, Mr. Notkiss began as usual to complain that he lived in a dark corner and his thoughts withered away due to his dearth of friends. At that very moment, a certain man was passing by wearing a short coat and a pressed hat, a parasol in hand, and greeted us in flowery German. Mr. Notkiss immediately jumped up happily and invited him to join us. But the man said self-deprecatingly, "I'm not worthy of this honor," and while he was speaking he leaned his parasol against the door and greeted Notkiss and bowed slightly to me and said, "I am Miefurst." I bowed my head before him and called out in wonder, "Ah, yes, translator of the poem 'The Shepherd Among the Lilies.'" Mr. Miefurst nodded his head again humbly and said, "Sir, you are correct." And he clasped my hand warmly and said, "Tiferet Yisrael's commentary on The Ethics of the Fathers was right when he claimed that Gutenberg, Johannes

Gutenberg who invented the printing press, deserves a place in the world to come. For someone like me lives in an isolated town and composes a poem – *a poem!* – and the poem gets published and is spread all over the world – *all over the world!* – and from this I acquire for myself dear friends and soul mates!" And while he was speaking Mr. Miefurst took out a handkerchief from his pocket and wiped his forehead. Red letters were embroidered on the handkerchief as a sort of monogram, and they took up a full quarter of the handkerchief. From all of his mannerisms it was apparent that Mr. Miefurst was a cultured man. And surely a cultured man like this was capable of guiding the thoughts of a young man seeking wisdom like Notkiss, who was perched on the threshold of knowledge, except that the dark thoughts in the hearts of youth erect a barrier between them and the rest of mankind.

Mr. Miefurst had lived his entire life in Pishevits and yet he was fluent in all the languages of Europe. They say that in his youth he didn't know even one foreign word, except for those used by Rashi, but when he was being supported by his wealthy father-in-law he bought himself Schulbaum's Hebrew-German dictionary and hadn't put it down until he'd memorized it. And this is how he did it: he divided up the dictionary into daily portions and every day he would learn one day's worth, like a person who recites the Psalms daily, one day to the next. In time, there was not a German word that was beyond his ken. And yet he still didn't know the correct pronunciation of any words, until the monarchy decreed that it was forbidden to take collateral against loans and whoever did so would be imprisoned, and he went to hide out at his dear friend the Swabian and learned from him how to pronounce the words properly, and when he got caught and was imprisoned he ordered himself a German-French dictionary and learned all the French words by heart. And from then on he would get a dictionary and study, get another dictionary and study, until he became fluent in all the languages. But of all the languages he chose to write only in German and French. German, because it had been the first stage in his education and French, out of respect for the French Revolution. He even translated the poem "The Shepherd Among the Lilies" from French into German.

Mr. Miefurst's company was very pleasant for me. We talked about Schiller and Sapir and the other great German poets. Mr. Miefurst knew at least several poems of each and every poet by heart. When I saw how capable he was, I started talking to him about trying to write in Hebrew. A man who was so proficient in cultured languages could surely bring untold good to our dismal literature whose readers wait with bated breath for the appearance of so much as a modern word. And he had no need to be ashamed for lack of companions. After all Dr. Doctor, even though he knows all the languages – even Ethiopian – nevertheless writes a great deal in Hebrew, as much as two European journalists. My words made an impression. Even though Mr. Miefurst was still busy at that time writing rules in German for the burial society, he agreed to try to put pen to paper in our holy language. I was reminded that it is written, "My own vineyard I have not kept," and I called out groaningly, "How can a man who has the power to make our language flourish carry on his work in the tongue of another nation?" And here Mr. Notkiss gestured to be silent, as Mr. Miefurst had already gotten what was coming to him in this world for writing those rules in foreign languages, inasmuch as the Hasids had befouled his seat in the synagogue with tar on the Day of Atonement. And so that he wouldn't feel embarrassed by his Hebrew author colleagues I reminded him how many doctors who had written their dissertations in German, as is generally done, are not among the slackers and yet now they write in Hebrew. I even passed along to him all the newly coined Hebrew words whose meanings had been modernized, words that the earlier modern Hebrew writers, who were immersed in the Bible and Talmud and medieval commentaries and research books were not privileged to have known.

Chapter Twenty-Five
The Shepherds' Tents

To make my father happy, I freed myself up from all my other affairs and went to see the rabbi. On the way I found an old woman holding two pitchers of milk, and I stopped and asked her how to get to the rabbi's home. The old woman put down her two pitchers and said, "You ask how to get to the rabbi's? Take yourself and go to the wide street and when you get to the wide street you will see two alleyways, one turning right and the other turning left. That being the case, you too turn yourself to the left. From this left alleyway you will get to the upper marketplace, and when you get to the upper marketplace you will right away see the butcher shop, but for God's sake do not turn into the butcher shop lest you transgress with its non-kosher meat. Rather, get yourself to the synagogue, and when you get to it you will immediately recognize it, and next to the synagogue you will find a rickety building, on the verge of collapse. That is the bathhouse, and next to it stands a row of public lavatories. Take yourself from there and go up the hill, where you will find three houses or maybe let's say four houses, and the house with the broken windows is the rabbi's house. But I will tell you, the hills of Pishevits are not like the hills of Vienna, for example, and there's no Jew who would be unable to point you to the rabbi's house." I said to her, "Grandmother, a nice landmark you've given me, broken windows, but perhaps they have fixed them?" And I added, "Grandmother, who was responsible for breaking the windows of the rabbi's house? Was it the at the hands of the Gentiles?" The old woman sighed and said, "No, rather at the hands of Jews, the Belzer Hasids. I said to her, "And they haven't fixed them, Grandmother?" She said to me, "My son, I'm certain they've already come back and re-broken them." I said to her, "Grandmother, is there no peace in this town?" She said to me, "My son, if only it was always like this." I said to her, "If that's so, what's this about them coming back and re-breaking them?" The old woman shook her head and sighed once again and said, "When our rabbi first came to town there was no peace here. Now, Praise God, there is peace in the town. Not just peace, but a wellspring of peace."

While we were talking a man came over and asked the old woman, "What does he want?" The old woman answered back, "He's asking for directions to the rabbi's house." The man said to her, "And so?" The old woman said, "And so, I told him which way to go." He said to her, "So why is he still standing here?" The old woman responded, "What does it matter to me?" The man said, "As usual, you haven't shown him properly." Said the old woman, "If you know a better way than what I've shown him, who's stopping you from showing him?"

I turned to the man and said, "The old woman showed me a good way, but I was asking her about the town's controversy." He said to me, "You want to know about the nature of the controversy, but after all it's an endless tale. But so what? We have time to tell you."

They don't say it that way in Szybusz. Rather they say, "Where are you running, do you think maybe the Strypa River's on fire?"

The man continued, "Perhaps you have a cigarette? You don't? Never mind. The truth is I don't smoke. Apparently it's possible to satisfy the need for tobacco just by smelling it. But let's get back to the original matter."

"You want to hear why there's no peace in the town, come I'll tell you. After the death of our old rabbi, of blessed memory, our town was left like a shepherdless flock. Not exactly like a flock without a shepherd because, after all, his rivals were still present, as was the rabbinical judge and all the others authorized to safeguard Jewish law, as it happens. Except that as the parable goes… Wait, what do I need a parable for, when the meaning itself is clear? And thus, our town was left like a flock without a shepherd. It didn't take long until the shepherds outnumbered the flock. There was not a study house that didn't have two rabbis. At first all of Pishevits followed Chortkov, but when the Belzer Hasids came into being, some people attached themselves to Chortkov and some attached themselves to Belz. And after the Belzer Rebbe married into the family of the Rebbe of Rachmanalitzlan, even the Hasids of Rachmanalitzlan came into their own. But even among the Hasids of Chortkov there is no peace, and the world has no idea how this quarrel will end."

"This quarrel, what was it about? After the death of the old rabbi, *may his merit shield us!*, Rabbi Yisraelneu took his place. As it is known, there is no one as wise as he in the whole world, an ancient sage, an expert in the Seven Wisdoms. They say he even knows how to read the newspapers. Even though I've been to Chortkov several times, I've never had the privilege of witnessing him read one. They say he reads in bed. And here I must wonder, for is it not forbidden to do anything after reciting the bedtime prayers, except he says that he reads at an hour which is neither day nor night. The long and the short of it is that during the reign of Rabbi Yisraelneu, may he live long, an enemy from within was created for him by God Himself. And who was it? Saraneu's husband. After all, he is the husband of the daughter of the eldest son of the old rabbi, and if the eldest son had been alive he would be sitting in the place of his father but now, since the eldest passed on, his son-in-law ought to rightfully be reigning in his place. As it is known, Saraneu's husband is no simpleton. I swear that I've seen his name written in a foreign language, both in print and in his own handwriting. Apparently, he amassed many followers and the world was split in two. And hence was born the great dispute. Belz wanted this rabbi and Rachmanalitzlan wanted that rabbi, some of Chortkov wanted this rabbi and other ones wanted the other. But finally our rabbi prevailed, the way King Saul slew his thousands. Whosoever opened his mouth against him was silenced by the rabbi with a coin of pure silver. A lucky man was our rabbi. Overnight he became rich. How so, overnight? This is what happened. One night thieves came to his house, not just any thieves but thieves with a wagon and two horses. The thieves stayed and loaded up the wagon with everything they could find in the house, his personal objects, his money, his wife's jewelry, and also monies that had been deposited with him by orphans and litigants, also silver and copper utensils that the poor had pledged to the rabbi's wife against loans with interest. As the thieves were getting ready to leave they detected an aroma of food cooking on the stove. Because our rabbi, *may he live long*, is frail, *God spare us*, after the midnight prayers he liked to eat something cooked by his wife, *may she live long*, in order to strengthen his body. The long and the short of it is that the thieves smelled the food and stayed to eat. And then, midnight arrived. The rabbi got up and stood for the midnight prayers, the thieves heard him and escaped, leaving behind the wagon and the horses. The rabbi and all the members of his household immediately went out and retrieved all the property and sold the wagon and horses for a lot of money, and from the proceeds he paid off his antagonists until he held his own in the town."

While he was still telling the story, a few of the people of Pishevits had gathered around. Another man up and challenged him, "Midnight prayers, he says? After all, your rabbi is from the Chortkov Hasids, and have you ever heard of Chortkov Hasids rising at midnight? Did your rabbi not say, 'We have already gotten past midnight?'" The first Jew mocked him and said, "If so, you go ahead and tell the story." The Belzer said, "It appears that I will tell it, why shouldn't I?" And the Chortkover responded, "Who's stopping you?" The Belzer said, "You think you can stop me?" The Chortkover said, "Heaven forbid." The Belzer said, "In that case, you should have been silent." The Chortkover said, "In the name of the Master of the Universe, I wish upon you the same strength to speak that I have." The Chortkover had not finished speaking when he began moaning and coughing and gurgling until both of his legs were trembling, indeed his whole body was trembling, his eyes were on fire and his arms extended and started twitching back and forth. The Chortkover groaned and shouted, "Alas, Jews, I haven't the strength to speak!"

The Belzer stuck all ten fingers into his beard, separating it into more and more tassels, and he said, "This was not what happened. Rather this is the way it happened. It wasn't your little rabbi who got up for the midnight service, but Pesach the Teacher his neighbor, and it was not for midnight prayers that he arose but rather to relieve himself. When Pesach saw the thieves, he began yelling. The rabbi went out and tried to pull the horses away from him, saying, 'Had the thieves not run away they would have stolen my money, and now that they've run away, to whom should the horses and wagon belong, tell me?' The rabbi was already fixing to pull the horses by their tethers when Pesach's wife jumped and said, *'Prrr!'* And she didn't let the rabbi get them. And the entire town agreed with her, not from loving Pesach but from disliking the rabbi. They said, 'It's enough that he got his belongings back.'"

One of those gathered asked, "And what did Pesach the Teacher do with his horses?" The Belzer peered at him and said, "You've asked an important question. Apparently, he didn't ride the town streets on them." Another interjected, "This man asked an appropriate question and you're brushing him off without any answer." The Belzer answered him, "He conferred with his friends and they asked him, 'Why are you keeping a horse and wagon? Better you should sell them and buy yourself a milk cow.'" A young man who was twirling his sidelocks said, "That was good advice they gave him." The Belzer fixed his gaze upon him and told him off. "Young pest, when your elders are talking, don't butt in." Said the young man, "Have I truly butted in?" The Belzer responded, "You should have kept quiet." The young man said, "I am being quiet." The Belzer, still derisive, said, "Better you should pay attention to your wife, who goes out with her hair uncovered." Someone else chimed in, "I'd hand that impertinent woman a certificate of divorce!" Another one said, "Phooey!" and spit. Someone else asked the Belzer, "And what ever happened with the cow?" The Belzer said, "What cow are you talking about?" He said, "The cow that Pesach the Teacher bought." The Belzer said, "First of all he didn't buy a cow and second of all he didn't sell his horses."

- "So then what did he do?"

- "Pesach said, 'I'll let them graze until the thieves repent for their actions and then I'll return to them what is theirs.' And he didn't hire out the horses, even for payment, a good deed."

- "And what happened in the end to the horses?"

- "If they're not dead yet, they're grazing in the meadow."

- "If so, how does that rabbi have money to pay off his antagonists?"

The Belzer responded, "Have your pleas for forgiveness for all of your sins been met, that you're now pleading for an answer to this as well?"

Chapter Twenty-Six
A Reason for Delay of the Redemption

The rabbi sat on a large chair reading the *Mahazikei HaDat* newspaper. His hat, a sable one, was leaning slightly to one side. When I entered he was startled and hid the newspaper and greeted me with the tips of his delicate fingers. I returned his greeting and sat across from him on the chair that he had cleared off for me, and he began to discuss with me the most pressing political issues and revealed to me his opinion that we were on the threshold of a great war. He was not of the same opinion as Nahum Sokolow who wrote in *HaTzfirah* that there would be no war, but that there is bound to be a great world war in the future for, if not, one would be denying, heaven forbid, the coming of the Messiah because otherwise what would be the purpose of the Armageddon that must presage the coming of the Messiah? I, being in the dark both about current publications and world affairs, diverted the conversation to a different matter, and I gave the rabbi regards from my father and told him what my father had said about Rabbi Hiyya and the Jerusalem Talmud. The rabbi stroked what remained of his beard after all of the altercations with the Belzer Hasids and said, "I will tell you something in the name of he who said it. The sage who wrote *The Redemption of Jacob* was, as is known, a great interpretive innovator and he included in his book many wonderful new interpretations, most of which were already found in the writings of the Rabbi Nissim of Gerona and other books of medieval sages. When they would say to him, 'Rebbe, this new interpretation in your book is already found in such-and-such book of such-and-such ancient sage,' he would say, 'I am exceedingly gratified that I have gone down the true path.' What is this parable similar to? To a man who is walking on the road and doesn't know if it's the right one. When he finds people there, he knows at once that he's on the right path." And the words of a wise man are gracious. I, too, cited the words of the sages to the Pishevits rabbi. I said to him, "The Vilna Gaon used to say, 'Why is it written, Of making many books there is no end?' The explanation of this is that the writing of many books delays the end of days by causing a postponement of the Redemption, as it is said in the Gemara, 'He who quotes a statement in the name of its author brings about Redemption to the world, but those who write many books and do not attribute their material to its originators delay Redemption.'"

As we were talking, an old man came in holding a broadside of paper. The old man asked the rabbi, while gesturing towards me, "Where is this young man from?" The rabbi said, "From Szybusz." The man with the poster looked me in the eye and asked, "From Szybusz?" I nodded back, "From Szybusz." The man looked me in the eye and said, "Incredible!" I said to him, "What's so incredible?" He said to me, "Indeed, we are brothers. Not that I am your brother or that you are mine, rather Moshe Chaim is my brother." I looked at that old man, with the long beard, unkempt side curls and stained clothes, and I remembered Moshe Chaim who wore a short coat, had a trimmed beard and not even a sign of side curls. The old one smiled and said, "I know you call him Moshe the Heretic. But you know what the Talmud says about calling someone by a bad nickname..." He hadn't had a chance to finish when the rabbi said, "Enough, Rabbi Elyakim." And he took the poster from Elyakim, its author, and said to me, "I heard about you that you write for their newspapers. Pray tell, is this rhetoric any good?" I took the broadside and I read:

With the Aid of the Exalted Almighty, etc., etc.
Important Warning:

To all of the holy community, please give heed. There is a new element amongst us, evil sinners who call themselves Zionists. They are Godless and postpone the end of days and they were not satisfied until they had organized a ball. Therefore, we have appointed ourselves as a rabbinic court to put a halt to this abomination and give warning to all Jews, men, women and children, not to set foot, God forbid, at the ball this evening and we thus shall have fulfilled the biblical injunction, as it is written, "Give glory to the Lord your God before darkness falls and your feet stumble on the hills of a *twilight ball.*"

Although the letters were large, it was difficult for me to read because they had stopped up the windows with colored pillows that blocked out the light. I got up and went over to the window. The rabbi got up and went over with me to the window and stood looking over my shoulder so as to relish the pleasant rhetoric. I hadn't yet been able to finish reading the entire warning before a rock was thrown into the house. The rabbi's wife cried out, "The last remaining pane of glass!" The rabbi said to me in a meek voice, "Please, can you take a look inside my mouth? I believe they've knocked out my last remaining tooth."

Chapter Twenty-Seven
The Ball

Announcements of the ball glistened from the walls of houses. Porters were carrying all sorts of benches and chairs on their shoulders, the flower of Zionist youth running after them with pictures of Zionist leaders in their hands. The youths were dressed in Sabbath clothes, ties wound round their necks with some sort of pins stuck in them, formed in the shape of the Star of David. The young ladies had arranged to have new dresses made for the ball and they were standing in front of the mirror, decorating their hair with some sort of scissor hair clips that they'd bleached white in the sun. Their mothers were assisting them and their fathers were running back and forth bringing them needle and thread or cosmetics. One person said to his friend, "Damn those Zionists! They are making balls. I'd like to know for what and for whom. For a month already my wife and daughters have been begging me day and night to get new dresses made for them and I still haven't finished paying for the old ones. Today the tailor delivered the dresses and wants to be paid in full. Where am I supposed to get the money to pay him? He keeps repeating, 'If you don't pay me, I'm not leaving the dresses.' I told the tailor, 'Here you are, here's my neck. Go ahead and slaughter me.' And he said, 'No money, no dresses.' I ran to the bank and it was closed. What's the special occasion? Mr. Cohen was practicing his speech for the ball and they had sprinkled a pile of sand on the floor so that he wouldn't be disturbed by passersby and his family is going around barefoot without shoes so that he doesn't hear the sound of their footsteps. I tried to force my way in. What did his wife do, but throw me off the stairs screaming, 'Wicked Jew! He'd better not get tripped up during his speech because of you!' However, Miefurst is remembered for the good, for if not for him I would have returned home penniless."

Another person began, "You haven't found yourself anyone to be remembered for the good besides Miefurst? *May his name and memory be obliterated!*" The borrower said to him, "What did Miefurst ever do to you? Just because he converses in German he deserves to die? Even so, I prefer him to a quorum of Zionists." The other responded, "And if he's better than ten Zionists that already makes him good in your eyes? And if he is good in your eyes, you think that makes him good? May fire spew forth from the Zionists and consume Miefurst, and may fire spew forth from Miefurst and consume the Zionists, and we'll be rid of the lot of them in one fell swoop."

Even though Pishevits blamed Zionism for delaying the end of days and for contradicting the premise that the Redemption of the Jews should be left in the hands of God and for causing a rise in heresy among the Jews, nevertheless the men of Pishevits did not prevent their daughters from going to the ball, since most of the young men during this time were Zionists and the fathers consoled themselves that after marriage the young men would forget about all their nonsense and become like everyone else. When the hour for the ball arrived there was no one in Pishevits that couldn't be found there, the young men on account of Zionism and the young women, as we have explained, and the mothers of the young women accompanied them, and their fathers stood outside holding the overcoats of their wives and daughters so that they would not catch cold upon leaving the hall. Even from all of the outlying villages of Pishevits came young men devoid of sidelocks but with waxed moustaches, and plump girls wrapped in silk and velvet and satin, whose garments could not contain their flesh. Even the Notkiss family came. Truly, the radiance of the Notkiss family had faded, inasmuch as from the day that Notkiss had been removed from his chairmanship all the Notkisses had lost their glory, and rather than hoping to ennoble Zionism by the honor of their presence, they looked forward to re-establishing themselves through Zionism. Whoever did not behold this ball, has never beheld a ball in all his days. The ball was held in a large hall, its walls were decorated with blue and white flags, and a large Star of David hung on the wall with a portrait of Herzl inside of it. The president of the association, Mr. Levi Cohen, welcomed everyone and gave a fine speech in which he compared the ball to Exile and Zionism to daylight, saying that just like daylight would follow the ball, in the same way Redemption would follow Exile. And when Mr. Levi Cohen stretched out his right hand towards the listeners and exclaimed, "Brothers, please heed our call – why should you be left like a dangling limb?" All hearts were elated and all eyes shed tears, and even Mr. Miefurst could not contain his tears and needed to make use of his handkerchief that was embroidered with red lettering. And the entire opening speech paled in comparison to Mr. Deixel's speech and they honored him greatly when they showered him with applause and called out, "Hooray!" until they split their lips.

The ball ended with the proper formalities and then the joy began to intensify and thin, long streamers of all kinds of paper, in all kinds of colors, began to be pulled to and fro around the hall encircling the young men and wrapping around the young women. At the same time, the young men waxed eloquent, first about the streamers, then about how hot it was and then about the ball. A young man said to a young woman, "Be so kind, Miss, as to look at this streamer that's entwining us together. Don't you think, Miss, that it's hot in here?" She answered and said, "I could stay here my whole life." The shy ones had to communicate by sending letters in the mail instead.

I also was rewarded for my efforts, as my article about the Pishevits ball was published in our Zionist newspaper, and in the same edition they also printed a picture of our Dr. David Davidsohn. Every time Dr. David Davidsohn would look at his image in the newspaper, he would see that his prophecy had been fulfilled: I had become a Jewish author.

The day after the ball, I returned to Szybusz. On the way to the train station, I ran into Mr. Deixel who had been accompanied in his departure by the whole town. He was holding an exceedingly beautiful and extraordinarily large bouquet of flowers that had been offered up to him by the daughters of Pishevits as a remembrance. I joined up with the Pishevitsers and went along with them.

Mr. Miefurst found me and was happy to see me and he took out a large sheet of paper and wiped his sweat with his wonderful handkerchief and began reading to me in a singsong cadence, "Poetry Inspired by the Holy Mountains," and he was walking alongside me reading me two rhyming stanzas that he had translated from German to Hebrew. He even used newly minted words in order to lend an air of elegance to his ancient tongue. Whoever has not beheld Mr. Miefurst reading has never beheld, in all of his days, an artist who takes pride in his work. Every so often he would point with his finger to this stanza or that verse in his poems and would stand looking at my face and examining me to see whether I had divined his intent, and then would read to me once again, until the sounds of the train were heard and it was time for me to board. I bade farewell to Mr. Miefurst and Mr. Notkiss and Mr. Levi Cohen and all my other friends in Pishevits and I climbed the steps into the train car with my dear friend Mr. Deixel and all the Zionists of Pishevits stood before us calling, "Farewell, farewell, farewell!"

One last drop of ink is left in the tip of my quill. As I stood at the window and gazed outside, I saw Alexander fettered in iron chains, being led away by an armed policeman. I don't know if it was by happenstance or whether Alexander had received his verdict in the Pishevits jail and was now being transferred to the prison in the provincial town, to await being returned to Russia.

I expressed my concern to Mr. Deixel and I said to him, "I'm afraid they might send him to Siberia." Mr. Deixel rested his nose on the bouquet of flowers in his hand and inhaled the scent, after which he placed his right hand on my shoulder affectionately and said, "Indeed, there is no complete joy in Exile."

The chains were ancient and were all rusted and were as red as blood. It appeared that the policeman was squeezing Alexander's hand so tightly that his blood was spattering onto the chains. But Mr. Deixel's flowers remained fresh and unwilted.

– Translated by Paul Pinchas Bashan & Rhonna Weber Rogol

Annotations to *Young and Old Together*

1. Young and Old Together / The story's title is taken from Exodus 10:9, but in fact is a reference to a poem by Y.L. Gordon by the same title (translated for the first time and appended to these annotations). The biblical resonance conveys the organic nature of the Jewish people, who confront Pharaoh in Egypt with the demand that "With our youth and with our elders we will go, with our sons and with our daughters, with our flocks and with our cattle we will go, for it is a festival of the Lord to us." Gordon's poem picks up that theme of Jewish unity and sets it as a response to a pogrom, and the power of anti-Semitism to unite different strands of the Jewish people. Agnon's story plays off of these sources, standing them on their heads, as he paints a satirical, opposite portrait of Jewish society in Galicia in 1907.

Y.L. Gordon

3. Davidsohn / Based on Dr. Nathan Birnbaum (1864-1937), who stood for election to the Austrian Parliament in the 1907 regional election representing Buczacz and the surrounding area. Supported by the Jews and Ukrainians, his election was thwarted by alleged corruption on the part of the Poles. Birnbaum was a journalist, writer, and thinker, who underwent a variety of phases in his life and career: starting as a nationalist (he coined the phrase "Zionism"), Yiddishist, advocate of Jewish cultural autonomy, and in his later years as a religious anti-Zionist. He was elected the first secretary-general of the Zionist Organization at the First Zionist Congress in 1897, as an advocate of cultural Zionism and an opponent of Herzl's political Zionism. Agnon may have given the character the name David Davidsohn as an allusion to "Messiah son of David," as a way of describing the Galician Jewish nationalist political aspirations.

Dr. Nathan Birnbaum

3. Szybusz / Agnon's literary name for his hometown Buczacz, located in eastern Galicia (today's western Ukraine). Pronounced "Shibush," the town name literally means mixed-up or muddled.

4. Deeds are not the essence / Inversion of the mishnaic principle, "It is not the study that is of the essence, but the deed" (Avot 1:17).

5. Itzhak Mundschpiel / Meaning of name: Laughing Mouth-play; i.e., a joker.

5. Adolph Stand / (1870–1919), Zionist leader and newspaper editor in Galicia and one of the leaders of world Zionism as an active organizer of Zionist societies. A noted orator and disciple of Herzl, although he favored practical settlement activity in *Eretz Yisrael*.

5. Men of truth who hate unjust gain / Exodus 18:21.

6. When the Pogroms Erupt / Judges 5:2.

6. Pishevits / Identified by Prof. Braver as Monasterzyska – a small town west of Buczacz.

6. Deixel / Meaning of name: *Di, ksil!* Enough, you fool!

7. It's not words that are of the essence / Avot 1:17.

7. Jewish National Fund / Founded at the Fifth Zionist Congress in 1901 to buy and develop land in Ottoman Palestine for Jewish settlement.

J.N.F. Collection Box

7. Graetz / Heinrich Graetz (1817-1891) was amongst the first historians to write a comprehensive history of the Jewish people from a Jewish perspective.

7. The Duke took hold of me… / Zevahim 96b.

7. Relief and deliverance / Esther 4:14.

8. Russo-Japanese War / February 1904-September 1905, fought over competing imperial ambitions in Manchuria and Korea.

Heinrich Graetz

8. Bund / The Jewish Labour Bund was a secular Jewish socialist party.

8. Mendele's *The Mare* / Sholem Yankev Abramovich (1836-1917), known by the penname Mendele Mocher Sforim ("The

Book-Peddler") was a Russian Jewish author and one of the founders of modern Yiddish and Hebrew literature. His satirical 1873 work *The Mare* depicts the Jew as a despised beast of burden, but one that maintains his moral superiority and inner dignity, much like Alexander to whom the narrator lends this book.

Mendele Mocher Sforim

8. A man's feet are responsible for him… / Sukkah 53a.

9. *HaTikvah* / "The Hope," anthem of the Zionist movement, and later the State of Israel, written by Naftali Harz Imber in 1877.

9. Singers got tripped up on a song / cf. Rosh HaShana 30b.

9. The hand is ready to shake the Lulav frond, but the beadle has locked the citron in his house / The Lulav (palm branch) and citron (Etrog) serve as implements of the Sukkot holiday prayers (see Leviticus 23:40).

10. The hands of Esau / Genesis 27:22.

11. Redder than the next / Sanhedrin 74a.

12. Sit still and do not act / Talmudic principle, here cynically misapplied, in which the Sages mandate inaction at the cost of not fulfilling a *mitzvah* in the face of possible transgression.

13. The Camp That Is Left Behind / Genesis 32:9.

13. The Infamous Maidservant / Cf. Lev. 19:20-22. Veixel misunderstands the name of the inn as a reference to a woman of ill repute. In the original Hebrew text Vovi explains how the inn received its unusual name, because of a mispronunciation and word play, unable to be captured in translation.

13. Veixel / Meaning of name: *Oy! You fool!*

13. "Bear Your Banner to Zion" / Zionist song written by Noach Rosenblum in 1898.

15. Through the Streets and Through the Squares / Song of Songs 3:2.

16. Chmielnicki / Bogdan Chmielnicki (c. 1595-1657), Cossack leader led revolt against Polish-Lithuanian Commonwealth,

Bogdan Chmielnicki

in the process initiated the 1648-1649 wave of pogroms decimating eastern European Jewry.

17. And It Is Said About the Nations / From the Rosh HaShana Musaf prayer of *Zichronot*.

17. *Voskhod* / Zionist Polish-language weekly (in Polish *Wschód*, meaning "The Dawn").

HaShachar

Moritz Gottlieb Sapir

17. *HaShachar* / 19th century Hebrew monthly, published in Vienna by Peretz Smolenskin.

17. Sapir / Moritz Gottlieb Sapir (or Saphir), 1795-1858, influential Viennese Jewish humorist and satirist.

17. Mr. Miefurst / In Hebrew as Mr. Ani VeAfsi Od ("I and no other"; cf Isaiah 47:8 and Zephaniah 2:15). A. Bar-Adon suggests this character is based on Eliezer Ben-Yehudah (1858-1922), known as the father of the revival of modern Hebrew.

17. Max Nordau / (1849-1923), was a Zionist leader, physician, author, and social critic. With Herzl he founded the World Zionist Organization and served as president or vice president of several Zionist congresses.

Max Nordau

R. Shmuel Mohilever

17. Rabbi Shmuel Mohilever / (1824–1898), a rabbi, pioneer of Religious Zionism and one of the founders of the Hovevei Zion movement.

17. Gershom Bader's yearbook / Bader (1868-1953) was an influential Hebrew and Yiddish literary and journalistic figure in Galicia. His short-lived Hebrew literary almanac, *HaHermon*,

was published in the first years of the twentieth century. Agnon briefly worked for Bader's newspaper *HaEt* in Lemberg, before it folded in 1907.

18. Leviathan and wild bull / According to rabbinic legend these will appear on the menu of the meal served to the righteous at the feast of the End of Days.

18. Sokolow's newspaper *HaTzfirah* / Nahum Sokolow (1859-1936) was a Zionist leader, author, translator, and pioneer of Hebrew journalism. He edited the Hebrew daily newspaper, *HaTzfirah*, which served as a platform for some of the greatest names in early modern Hebrew literature.

HaTzfirah

18. Fish mentioned in the Talmud / Shabbat 118b, s.v. *kasa de-harsana*.

18. Ahad Ha'am / Pen-name of Asher Ginsberg (1856–1927), journalist, essayist, and preeminent Zionist thinker; founder of "cultural Zionism" aiming toward the establishment of a "Spiritual Center" as opposed to Herzl's political Zionism. The pen-name Ahad Ha'Am (taken from Genesis 26:10) means "one of the people."

Ahad Ha'am

19. Bloch and Bick / Yosef Shmuel Bloch (1850-1923) was a rabbi, writer, and three-term deputy of the Austrian parliament from 1884. Dr. Emil Bick of Lemberg was a political rival to Bloch.

19. A woman will suffer frugal living… / Mishnah Sota 3:4: "R Yehoshua says: A woman prefers merely one measure [i.e., living frugally] and licentiousness [i.e., frequent sexual relations], rather than nine measures [i.e., luxury] and chastity."

19. Money solves everything / Ecclesiastes 10:19.

20. Tintenfass / Meaning of name: German for ink-pot.

21. Doctor Shebishifleinu… / Meaning of name: "The lowest among us," cf. Psalms 136:23.

21. Sternhimmel and Himmelstern Tzigenmilch and Nachtmahl / Starry heaven; heavenly star; goat milk; and evening meal.

23. Goldmann Circle / Nation-wide Jewish assimilationist group in Poland, founded by Bernard Goldmann (1842-1901); thanks to Mr. Rafi Weiser for help in making this identification.

Bernard Goldmann

23. For the sake of Zionism… / cf. Isaiah 62:1.

23. Utopians like Bellamy / A reference to Edward Bellamy's 1888 utopian novel *Looking Backward*, a worldwide best-seller which created a political mass movement, with a profound socialist impact.

23. Suchard chocolate / Swiss brand of chocolate, the Suchard company was the largest producer of chocolates in Europe at the end of the 19th century.

CHOCOLAT SUCHARD

Suchard Chocolate

24. "The Tip of the *Yud*" / 1875 Hebrew epic poem by Y.L. Gordon "*Kotzo shel Yud*," among the best-known works of the Hebrew Enlightenment, is a sharp satire of the status of women within Judaism. Translated and with an introduction by Stanley Nash, "The Tip of the *Yud*," *CCAR Journal* 53:3 (Summer 2006), pp. 107-188.

24. Jacob Gordin / (1853-1909) Russian-born Yiddish playwright and journalist. In his ignorance Deixel is confusing Jacob Gordin with Y.L Gordon.

25. *Götz Krafft* / 4-volume German bildungsroman (1904-05) by Edward Stilgebauer (1868-1936).

25. *Degeneration* by Max Nordau / 1892 moralistic attack on so-called degenerate art,

Jacob Gordin

as well as a polemic against the effects of a range of the rising social phenomena of the period, such as rapid urbanization and its perceived effects on the human body

25. Alfred Nossig / (1864–1943), Polish Jewish sculptor, musician, writer, and Zionist activist. His epic poem called "*Jan Prorok*" (John the Prophet) was written in 1892.

Alfred Nossig

26. Terror in the City / Jeremiah 15:8.

28. Kortitschnikivitz / Meaning of name is a joke, taking the Yiddish *kort*, meaning playing card, and turning it into a Polish-sounding family name.

30. Night of *Hoshana Rabba* / According to tradition the final night of the Sukkot holiday is spent studying Torah until daybreak.

31. An Unattended Corpse / Halakhic concept, *met mitzvah*, in which the tending to the final disposition and burial of the dead, especially when no other person is available to do so, takes precedence over all other obligations. Colloquially used to describe a situation of suddenly chancing upon an unattended corpse.

31. Oh and alas to that kind of drinking / In the Hebrew text the character is referring to a "*tikkun*," a ceremony at which one imbibes ritually commanded spirits at the study house on the anniversary of a relative's death or to ward off illness, with the emissary of the Hasidic Rabbi portioning out spirits to his followers.

32. Purification board / Plank on which the deceased is ritually washed in preparation for burial.

32. Oberschenkil / Meaning of name: Upper thigh; alt. from the Yiddish *schenk*, meaning tavern the name becomes: master bartender.

34. Kreutzer / A small copper coin of the Austro-Hungarian Empire.

Kreutzer

35. Lilien / Ephraim Moses Lilien (1874–1925) was an art nouveau illustrator and print-maker particularly noted for his art on Jewish and Zionist themes. He is sometimes called the "first Zionist artist" and was involved in the founding of the Bezalel Art School in Jerusalem.

Illustration by Lilien for the 5th Zionist Congress (1901)

36. *Sefer HaYuhasin* / Historical work recounting Jewish and world history from Creation through the late 15th century by Abraham Zacuto (1452-1515), mathematician, rabbi and historian who served as Royal Astronomer to King John II of Portugal.

36. Pope Joan / According to legend (regarded as a fiction by modern scholars), Joan reigned as pope for a few years during the Middle Ages. Her story first appeared in 13th century chronicles and subsequently spread widely through Europe.

37. Rinaldo Rinaldini / "Penny-dreadful" German novel by C.A. Vulpius (a brother-in-law of Goethe), *Rinaldo Rinaldi, The Robber Captain* (1797).

C.A. Vulpius

39. Strife Among Brothers / Proverbs 6:19.

39. Raumer's book about girls' education / Karl Georg von Raumer (1783-1865), German geologist and educator, wrote *Die Erziehung der Madchen* (translated as *The Education of Girls*, 1816).

39. Second / In the codes of dueling, a "second" (friend or agent of each aggrieved party) would attempt to resolve a dispute upon acceptable terms, or in the event negations fail, they would arrange and oversee the details of the "encounter" (the duel).

39. I shall go in your place / cf. Samuel II 19:1.

40. Go out and behold / Song of Songs 3:11.

41. Gulden and krone / The Austro-Hungarian Gulden was replaced by the Krone in 1892 at a rate of 2 Krone for each Gulden.

43. Moses Nuts / In Yiddish "*Rebbi's nissel*" (the Rebbe's nut) was a nickname for peanuts, possibly due to the presence of what looks like a bearded face when the nut is split carefully. Prof. Avraham Holtz reports that calling them *Moishe rabbeinu's nisselakh* (Moses' nuts; i.e., the Rebbe *par excellence*) was a Lemberg regional variation.

47. *Ost und West / East and West* was a German language magazine of Jewish culture (Berlin, 1901-1923) meant to bridge the German Jewish world with Eastern European Jewry.

Ost und West

48. Yoav and Shimmi / Bava Batra 21b and Maharsha: The narrator has confused Shimi for David in an incident in 1 Kings 11:16, in which Yoav (David's general) kills all the Edomite males (*zachor*) due to a misreading of the verse in Deut. 25:19, "You shall blot out the remembrance (*zecher*) of Amalek."

48. Morris Rosenfeld and Sholem Asch / Rosenfeld (1862-1923) was a Yiddish poet; emigrated from Poland to New York in 1886, where his poetry often depicted the life of Jewish emigrants, especially those in the garment industry. Asch (1880-1957) was a Polish-born American Jewish novelist, dramatist, and essayist in Yiddish.

Sholem Asch

49. Heine's poem / Heinrich Heine (1797-1856), the Enlightenment's most famous Jewish apostate, was a German poet, journalist, essayist, and literary critic. His 1851 poem "Jehuda Ben Halevy" deals with the theme of longing for Jerusalem.

Heinrich Heine

49. Reuben Brainin / (1862-1939) was a Russian Jewish publicist, biographer and literary critic.

49. *HaShiloah* / Monthly Hebrew journal founded by Asher Ginsberg (Ahad Ha'Am) in 1896, covering Jewish life, literature and culture.

50. *Cudze chwalicie…* / Well known Polish ditty by Stanisław Jachowicz (1796-1857), educator and author of books for children.

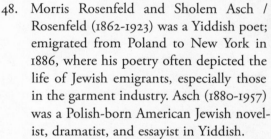
HaShiloah

51. Gymnastics club / Hebrew text refers specifi-
cally to the Sokół (Polish Gymnastic Society), the oldest youth movement in Poland.
Created in 1867, the group's goal was to
develop fitness, both physically and mentally.

Sokół Gymnastic Club

53. D'Annunzio / Gabriele D'Annunzio (1863-1938), Prince of Mon-
tenevoso, was an Italian writer, poet, journalist, playwright and
soldier during World War I. He occupied a prominent place
in Italian literature and political life.

53. *The Sunken Bell* by Gerhart Hauptmann / An 1896 German
poetic play in blank verse by Gerhart Hauptmann (1862-1946),
Nobel laureate in literature in 1912.

53. Sephardic and Ashkenazic pronunciation / The adoption of
Sephardic pronunciation for modern Hebrew was a point of
controversy. The fact that the traditionalist Hasids follow the
prayer text customs of the Sephardic (or Lurianic) tradition
notwithstanding, they maintained the Ashkenazic pronunciation of those prayers – a point lost on Mr. Deixel.

54. Hebrew school / Part of the Zionist initiative in reviving Hebrew
involved the establishment of schools to teach Hebrew or where
instruction would be conducted in Hebrew.

54. *Tsafra tava! Ramsha tava!* / Aramaic for "Good morning! Good
evening!" Agnon is being ironic: in fact the Hebrew accomplishment is empty, as the girls are speaking Aramaic (a Jewish dialect
of ancient Palestine and Babylonia during Talmudic times).

55. Ya'avetz / Hebrew acronymic for Jacob ben Tzvi Emden (1687-
1776), was a leading German rabbi and Tal-
mudist; leading opponent of the Sabbatean
false-messianic movement.

55. Ze'ev Yavetz / (1847-1924) was an educator
and historian; born in Russia he emigrated
to Zikhron Yaakov in 1887. The school
director, in his ignorance, cannot differen-
tiate between Ya'avetz and Yavetz.

56. Uganda / 1903 proposal to create a Jewish homeland in a portion of British East

Ze'ev Yavetz

Africa. The plan created a major schism within the larger Zionist movement, drawing support from Herzl, and opposition from Menachem Ussishkin and others. Ultimately rejected at the 1905 Seventh Zionist Congress.

56. Ahasver / The legendary wandering Jew, who taunted Jesus on the way to the Crucifixion and was then cursed to walk the earth.

56. My own vineyard have I not kept / Song of Songs 1:6; meaning here that he was clean-shaven.

56. The teacher has prevailed / In the Hebrew text Deixel states, "The teacher has prevailed at Sedan" – a reference to the 1870 Battle of Sedan at which the Prussian army decimated the French forces, a victory which was credited to the education provided by the military instructors, thus: It was the teachers who prevailed at Sedan. The school director, victorious in this particular debate, may very well have served in the Prussian forces, or Diexel may merely be using a turn of phrase which would have been known at the time. Thanks to Prof. Hillel Weiss for successfully identifying this enigmatic source.

57. Textbook / This translation has excised a paragraph with multiple Hebrew word-plays; ironically, the proof they are bringing for proper Hebrew pronunciation is actually about a Polish word.

57. Columbus's egg / Apocryphal tale first recorded in Girolamo Benzoni's *History of the New World* (1565): "Columbus was dining with many Spanish nobles when one of them said: 'Sir Christopher, even if your lordship had not discovered the Indies, there would have been, here in Spain, which is a country abundant with great men knowledgeable in cosmography and literature, one who would have started a similar adventure with the same result.' Columbus did not respond to these words but asked for a whole egg to be brought to him. He placed it on the table and said: 'My lords, I will lay a wager with any of you that you are unable to make this egg stand on its end like I will do without any kind of help or aid.' They all tried without success and when the egg returned to Columbus, he tapped it gently on the table breaking it slightly and, with this, the egg stood on its end. All

those present were confounded and understood what he meant: that *once the feat has been done, anyone knows how to do it.*"

59. Kraindel Tscharney / A main character in Agnon's 1912 novella *And the Crooked Shall Be Made Straight* (forthcoming in English from The Toby Press). She is an "abandoned wife" as her husband is declared dead, incorrectly, so that when she remarries and gives birth to a son, the father our story's Mr. Hofmann, the child and his descendants are all halakhically *mamzerim* (bastards), unbeknownst to anyone in town, but known to us, the readers of the tale.

1912 Hebrew edition of *And the Crooked Shall Be Made Straight*

59. Travails / The calamities set to befall the world prior to the advent of the Messiah (see Sanhedrin 98b).

60. *Lag BaOmer* / The 33rd day of the seven week Omer period between Passover and Shavuot; observed as a joyful but minor festival.

60. Empty house and a money bag full of holes / cf. Haggai 1:6.

62. Strypa / River that runs through Buczacz (i.e., Szybusz); a tributary of the Dnister.

Strypa River in Buczacz

62. Sebastian Montag / Considered to be based on Berish Stern (mayor of Buczacz, 1879-1921). Montag makes appearances in Agnon's *A Simple Story*, and is referenced in *A Guest for the Night* as well.

65. Hemdat / Here we learn the name of the narrator for the first time – Hemdat, a recurring character in Agnon's writing, widely understood to be an autobiographical projection of the author into his work. See, e.g., his appearances in the novel *Only Yesterday*, as well as the autobiographical story "Hemdat" forthcoming in English in *Forevermore* (The Toby Press).

65. 'Rabbi Gadiel the Infant' or 'The Tale of the Woodchopper' or 'The Legend of the Messiah' / All early Agnon stories.

66. Kishinev pogroms / Anti-Jewish riots in the capital of the province of Bessarabia in the Russian Empire (now the capital of the Republic of Moldova), on April 19-20, 1903, and a second, smaller riot in October 1905.

Burying desecrated Torah scrolls following Kishinev pogrom

68. Seek the welfare of the city… / Jeremiah 29:7.
68. Honor the physician… / Various *midrashim* according to Ben Sira 38:1.
69. Rabbi Meir of Premishlan / Hasidic rabbi (1783-1850).
69. I will bring a nation… / Jeremiah 5:15.
69. *HaMagid* / First Hebrew weekly newspaper, published in Germany, then later in Poland and Vienna, between 1856-1903.

HaMagid

70. Sixty men cannot overtake / Bava Kama 92b.
70. First nine days of Av / Mournful period of nine days leading up to the fast of the Ninth of Av, commemorating the destruction of the Jerusalem Temples. During these nine days meat and wine are not consumed.
71. Przybyszewski / Stanisław Feliks Przybyszewski (1868-1927) was a Polish novelist, dramatist, and poet of the decadent-naturalistic school. His drama is associated with the Symbolism movement. He wrote both in German and in Polish. "The Snow" was a 1903 drama.
73. Chazermeyrinski's or at Schweintochinski's / Names playing off associations with pigs.
75. On That Night Hath Fled the Sleep / Esther 6:1.
75. Grandfather / The details of the grandfather character (referred to here as Rabbi Yakir) align with the biography of Agnon's maternal grandfather, R. Yehudah HaCohen Farb, an important town leader in Buczacz and powerful influence on the author's young

R. Yehudah Farb

life. He is depicted in a wide variety of Agnon's stories, from those relating nostalgic childhood recollections to the surrealistic tales of *Sefer HaMa'asim*.

76. Ninth of Av / *Tisha B'Av*, mournful day commemorating the destruction of both the first and second Temples of Jerusalem.

77. Age of upheaval / Deuteronomy 32:20.

77. You shall meditate upon it day and night / Joshua 1:8.

77. Shalmaneser / 8th century BCE Assyrian king, conqueror of Northern Kingdom of Israel (1 Kings 17-18).

77. Joseph Della Reina / 15th century Spanish rabbi and kabbalist, whose attempts to hasten the redemption became a thing of legend. Agnon's first published work, at around the age of 14, was a 1903 Yiddish poem about Della Reina. Prof. Arnold Band describes Agnon's thirty-stanza ballad as the story of the mystical rabbi "who tried to subdue the devil and almost succeeded in doing so before he was cheated of his success. To be sure, the poem is primarily of historical interest, but there is a charm in the childish naiveté of the verses which carry the story along with a pleasant melody, unquestionably in the tradition of popular Yiddish poetry."

77. Lilith / Mythological character, often portrayed as a female demon, in demonic terms.

77. Mountains of darkness / Tamid 32b identifies a possible location of Gehinnom as "behind the Mountains of Darkness."

79. Kiddush and Havdalah / Blessings recited over a cup of wine at the onset and conclusion of the Sabbath.

81. Marriage contract / *Ketubah*; according to the Talmud a man cannot live with his wife in the absence of a marriage contract.

82. Mohr / (1815-1868), Lemberg-born scholar and Haskalah figure, wrote in Hebrew and Yiddish, and a harsh critic of traditional rabbinic figures. His *Shvilei Olam* (*The Paths of the World*) was published 1856.

84. Rabbi Binyamin / Pseudonym of Yehoshua Radler-Feldmann (1880-1957), Hebrew journalist, educator, and religious Zionist.

Yehoshua Radler-Feldmann

Born in Galicia, Rabbi Binyamin arrived in Palestine in 1907, where he met and befriended Agnon.

85. Golden Book of JNF / Honor roll book of donors to the Jewish National Fund. The book was initiated in 1901 and is still on display (today in many multiple volumes) at the JNF headquarters in Jerusalem.

87. Chortkov / Town in western Ukraine, about 35 km. east of Buczacz, center of the Chortkov Hasidic dynasty (of which Agnon's father was a member).

87. A person should only take leave... / Berakhot 31a.

88. If they would bring me mushrooms... / Berakhot 47a: "If two individuals ate a meal together and a third came to eat with them, as long as the two are willing to eat more, the third may join them for the Grace after meals, in accordance with the opinion of Samuel."

89. Tiferet Yisrael / Tiferet Yisrael (Boaz) to Avot 3:1.

90. Schulbaum / Moses Schulbaum (1830-1918) was a linguist and scholar of the Hebrew language, his *Neues, vollständiges deutsch-hebräisches Wörterbuch* was first published in 1881.

90. Swabia / Region of southwestern Germany.

91. Dr. Doctor / In the first edition of the story this character was named Dr. Klausner. Joseph Klausner (1874-1958), was a historian and professor of Hebrew Literature, as well as the losing candidate in the first Israeli presidential election. Agnon and Klausner were Jerusalem neighbors, and had a famously chilly relationship, as depicted in *A Tale of Love and Darkness*, the memoir of Klausner's nephew, Amos Oz.

Joseph Klausner

92. The Shepherds' Tents / Song of Songs 1:8.

94. Rachmanalitzlan / Meaning of name: *Heaven's mercy!*

94. Saul slew his thousands / 1 Samuel 18:7.

95. Midnight prayers / *Tikkun Hatzot*; mournful petitions recited at midnight by the pious in longing for Redemption.

98. *Mahazikei HaDat* / Hebrew newspaper published in Galicia between 1879-1914, surveying Orthodox Jewish life.

Mahazikei HaDat

99. Of making many books / Ecclesiastes 12:12.

100. Give glory to the Lord your God before darkness falls and your feet stumble on the hills of a *twilight ball* / Jeremiah 13:16, playing off the fact that *neshef* means "twilight" in Biblical Hebrew, but was adopted to mean "ball" (an evening celebration) in modern Hebrew.

102. Fire spew forth... / cf. Judges 9:15.

104. Poetry Inspired by the Holy Mountains / cf. Psalms 87:1.

104. One last drop of ink is left in the tip of my quill / cf. Midrash Tanhuma – Ki Tissa 20.

— Annotated by Jeffrey Saks

With Our Young and Our Old We Shall Go
Y.L. Gordon

With Our Young and Our Old We Shall Go

One nation have we been, and thus shall we remain,
Carved out from one deep quarry;
Fused in joy and, too, in pain
A two millennia exile story
Land to land, both to and fro,
With our young and our old we shall go.

In the course of life, man closes off from any other's need,
Each tends to his own pasture, looking neither left nor right.
His friend he treats like dirt, he casts his brother at his feet,
For a man forsakes companions to save himself from blight;
Yet when our Lord's voice calls out, and summons us, behold
We shall go then, with our young and our old.

"There exists here a fifth column, with a penchant to inform,
They abide by different statutes, will they keep the kingdom's law?"
'Tis a lie you are pronouncing! We were loyal and conformed,
We are Israelites, we grant you, and our Torah hold in awe,
Yet when the king's commandment calls us, even so
With our young and our old we shall go.

Young and Old Together

We are one people, with one Lord,
Carved out from one deep quarry,
Interwoven with this triple cord,
Books of Torah, Hebrew's glory,
Bound together by these ties, chains of purest gold,
We shall go then, with our young and our old.

The elders and the young ones – some wealthy and some wise,
With the passing of the years, old and young will heed the call
To rally towards our holy flag, together we'll arise
Like the frailest of the flock, come the whirling of the squall
The storm that won't distinguish 'tween the highest and the low,
With our young and our old we shall go.

Though the storms whirl and the winds seethe tomorrow,
And you're up to your necks in the turbulent water –
Fear not, O Jacob, stoop not low in sorrow.
Human hordes will not take you to bloodshed and slaughter!
From the tempest cries out our Lord, oh so bold –
We shall go then, with our young and our old.

We'll hold fast to the Lord, not abandon belief,
His language of holiness will stay on our tongue,
We've witnessed some evil, but will see no more grief,
We'll live on in this land, as we always have done.
Even if God has finished, still no need to forego –
With our young and our old we shall go.

– Translated by Rhonna Weber Rogol

Chapters from
The Book of State

Orange piles at Damascus Gate, Jerusalem, May 1944 (Library of Congress American Colony Collection)

Introduction

FOR AS LONG AS I CAN REMEMBER I have meant to document the deeds of the State in a book. Yet I recoiled with each attempt. For the State is not like other living entities that inspire the writer, moving him to write with benevolence or malevolence. Neither is the State a random gathering of people, a fraternity or group of groups that happen to be in a single place, so that the competent scribe can sketch them out with a single flourish of his quill. Rather, the State is a metaphysical concept rendered into something physical which feigns meta-physicality. When you attempt to approach it as a metaphysical entity it slips back into physicality; if one considers it in physical terms it suddenly reverts into meta-physicality. If the writer should abandon hope of capturing the multifaceted nature of the State in a single account, and wishes to suffice with the depiction of a single facet, what does that selfsame facet do? That facet takes on a new façade, shows a different face, one of endless, infinite faces, each with a hidden and revealed dimension, so that none can be certain of its true face, of its essence. It is therefore no wonder that I recoiled at the task. Yet the idea of recording the deeds of the State continued to haunt me; though I despaired of ever writing the book, the book never despaired of being written. Many a time I was struck by a vision of blank pages rustling in the wind, each page crying like a soul stripped bare – "Have you no Hebrew words to clothe us in?"

I translated this mystical plea into plain language: namely, that I must fill in the blank pages myself. "Why me?" I asked, "Does the State lack ink-slingers?" Came the answer: "There is no lack thereof." "If so," I pressed, "let them write about the deeds of the State." They replied how they replied.

I checked what all these writers had been writing and found their words quite pathetic, profuse in praise for the State but without any real depiction of the State. I assume that this trick was learned from the speech-makers, and I say: what becomes a speaker does not become a writer; if it's pathos you're after, speeches are quite sufficient.

Yet still I stayed my hand from writing, for this only heightened my awareness of my inability to remove matters from their literal context and discuss them on a philosophical level. As you well know I only write about what I see with my own eyes, but (as noted above) the State is brimming with faces and facets, endless and infinite, not to mention its ungraspable, perpetually shifting concepts which themselves encompass changes upon changes. All this was excuse enough to wash my hands of the task. But the idea to encapsulate the deeds of the State in writing continued to nudge me, so I said to myself: Necessity dictates that I write the book, and if I cannot write the deeds of the State itself, I shall record the deeds of its leaders.

And once I again, I met with drawbacks and pitfalls, for even the State leaders wear many different faces. Yesterday they appeared like this, and today they appear like that, with their faces changing in between and all the while, according to the needs of the moment and the needs of the State. Furthermore, I saw that in order to record the ways of the State leaders, a writer must have certain fixed notions, while I have yet to reach this rank; because everything I perceive, I also perceive its opposite. And through this double vision, I find that both positions appear one and the same to me, so that my words leave as much room for doubt as if I were one of those tired pandering yes-men.

So I despaired even of this task, that is, to record the deeds of the State leaders. I gave into my despair and declared, What others have written is enough for me. Yet I could not resign myself to defeat; when I flipped through those books again I saw that their flamboyant praises left no room for actual substance. They melted under scrutiny, like proud ice sculptures (carved in honor of their inauguration) that melt under the sun's gaze. Something in my heart murmurs to me, urging me, *write*. Moreover, this selfsame heart suddenly gathers courage and asks me to write about the State itself, revving me to overcome all obstacles and doubts; to apply myself to the task and record a little of what my eyes have seen. By no means have they seen it all; some matters certainly demand further sight. But I can honestly say that I have written only what my own eyes have seen, which is no small virtue among this generation of writers. So this book may serve as eyes for future writers who wish to inscribe the deeds of the State themselves, and I hope that my actions will move others to do as I have done, for, more often than not in this State, when a person does something, others soon follow in his wake. And no wonder, for the shopkeeper who sells me a bit of ink and paper can't make a living from my purchases alone. As for the idea, which is entirely mine, nature dictates that every entity casts a shadow.

While I have tried with all my might to record things as they are, when it came to reporting the dialogue I was forced to adapt its style, as most of the State's great ones mix up their language and employ archaic rhetoric that strays from its true meaning, and sometimes they state the opposite of what they mean. Even their everyday speech is suffused with fabricated words, which they flaunt, declaring, "see how many hundreds of words I've invented!" The author of this book, who carefully weighs each word and consonant, challenges these word-spinners with an adage ascribed to Augustus Caesar: "I rule over the entire Roman Empire, but I cannot invent a single Roman word." Due to their pompous rhetoric and fabricated lexicons, these leaders' words are liable to be forgotten within half a generation – for their content will become inaccessible to their readers – so I have rendered their speech into plain, simple language; that which has been spoken before us, and shall be spoken for generations to come.

Before I take my leave of this book, I wish to repel certain slander it has subjected me to; accusations that ever since the publication of the chapter "The Kidnappers" the number of kidnappings in the State has risen alarmingly. I deny that this is so; I am not to blame and my words are not to blame; rather, the generation is to blame. Even if it is claimed that the written word is eventually fulfilled, the end of the book of Judges sees the Benjaminites seizing women for wives – yet the generations since have not seen their imitators seizing women without dowries. Yet they still complain about me as if I had indoctrinated my contemporaries in the art of kidnapping.

> *To conclude, a prayer for the welfare of State*
> *And the ministers who upon her wait*
> *Their noble words have my own inspired*
> *By their stately pride this book is fired*
> *As deep as a nail hammered into the wall.*
> *I lay down my pen. May God save us all.*

– Translated by Sara Daniel

The Kidnappers

THE MEETING HALL WAS FULL TO CAPACITY. Not a person in town failed to come, because the State was in the grip of major crises and no one knew what to do about them. Since Mr. Schreiholz was to be the speaker, the city's entire population turned out. For the custom of this State is that nothing is done without first deliberating upon it, and deliberation means speakers and orators. Once the speeches have been made and the orations delivered, the citizens of the State believe they have done something. If the crisis passes, well and good, if it does not pass another speech is made. Until a more serious crisis arises and a different orator is called upon. If the crisis passes, well and good, and if it does not pass, etc., etc.

People are pleased by these public assemblies where they gather in unity, where speeches are delivered, and where a person is thus led to feel that he has taken some action. There are some who know in advance everything that the speaker is going to say, and there are others who, even after the speaker has concluded his speech, do not know what he said. And there are still others who do not care what is said so long as they pass away two or three hours of their lost and desolate lives. They fear the moment when the speaker will conclude his address and they will return home to find their wives tired, since the wives also had attended the same meeting. Even though every speech is followed by a reception in honor of the speaker, not everyone is privileged to be among the invitees. Looking at that crowd of people one might believe them to be homogeneous, but the fact is that each and every person is like a nation unto itself. On the other hand, as to the women, each is like a race unto itself, even though their hair, the color of their faces, and everything else that testifies to a person's race were made up by the same artisan.

The time came for Mr. Schreiholz to begin. However, in accordance with the practice of all experienced speakers, he generally arrived late, sometimes half an hour, sometimes a full hour. But as to the audience, it generally arrived early, because everybody wanted to find a good seat, or to say a few words to his neighbor, since every person's ego flatters him and tells him, "You too have something to say and you should say it." If a person exhausts his topic of conversation, he proceeds to repeat what he has said yesterday and the day before. And if a person gets bored by his neighbor's words he does not really mind. In fact he feels flattered when he sees that his neighbor's wisdom is no greater than his own. The leaders and community workers who were in attendance out of respect for Schreiholz sat there, annoyed, as people are who see someone else doing what they themselves should have done. As they sat they looked around at the photos on the walls of the meeting house. In their imagination they even saw themselves as if their own portrait already graced the wall, and they thus tasted a morsel of immortality, similar to the immortality earned by their deceased colleagues.

Few are those who have no desire for immortality, especially among government officials and wielders of authority, because their ideal self-image is co-mingled with how they feel physically, and how they feel physically does not live up to their ideal self-image. But since they more or less resemble those who have already attained immortality, they have logical justification for believing that they too deserve immortality. However, this concept of immortality is not a corporeal concept, therefore nobody is much concerned with finding out the extent of this immortality and when it is decreed, whether with the cessation of the heartbeat or with the closing of the grave.

The audience began to be impatient and the air began to thicken. Nobody knew why he was sitting there, and what words he expected to hear. But it had become habitual to assemble and listen to speeches, and that which becomes a community habit is never questioned. But in the meantime people do exchange some comments about the situation.

For example, a woman said to her neighbor that a window should be opened. The neighbor replied: "I am sorry, lady, but I am unable to fulfill your request." "Why not?" "Because all the windows are open." She looked at him angrily and asked, "Why then is it so hot in here?" He answered: "The breeze that comes in through one window goes out through the window facing it."

Another person declared: "Schreiholz is late, he may not get here." To which another replied: "Perhaps he is still working on the preparation of his speech." To which the first one answered: "I wish he did prepare, so that he would know what he is talking about." His neighbor looked at him as if his very own thoughts had been stolen from him. However, since people generally do not say what they really think, he switched and said, "A speaker like Schreiholz is not really in need of that." To which another replied, "But we are in need of it." Then another person declared: "You are naive my friend if you believe that people do what they are supposed to do." Someone looked at his watch and asked, "Well, when will he begin?" Another whispered in his ear, "What difference does it make to you whether he begins or does not begin?" To which the first person replied, "Perhaps you are right." The second responded: "You say perhaps I am right, and I tell you I have never been so right as just now. Any way, Schreiholz should be urged to hurry and get here."

Just then three young men came to Mr. Schreiholz's home. When he saw their clothes he was puzzled. What do people dressed in such old and wrinkled clothes want with him? But Schreiholz had a good trait: he saw everything that had any relationship to him as intended for his good and for his pleasure. "They are probably representatives of the people," he thought. He extended a friendly greeting to them, saying: "Well my friends, I guess you have come to call for me." "Yes, Mr. Schreiholz," the young men replied, "we have come to call for you. We have a car waiting for you outside."

He placed a thick cigar in his mouth and accompanied the young men. On the way out he looked into the mirror and straightened out his mustache. Continuing in his friendly manner toward the young men he said, "Well, I guess the assembly hall is full!" "Filled to overflowing," the young men replied. "And what about the lobby?" "People are standing jammed together and waiting for you, sir," the young men replied. Mr. Schreiholz got into the car, crossed his legs, and wrapped himself in clouds of cigar smoke. He was in good spirits, with a sense of pride familiar to experienced speakers when an audience awaits them. And if any thoughts can be ascribed to Mr. Schreiholz, it is probable that he was thinking as follows: I will enter the assembly hall and the entire audience will rise in my honor. I shall bounce up the stairs to the platform, or perhaps I will not bounce up but rather walk up slowly, place my watch in front of me, look out upon the audience, with the entire audience straining its ears to listen, so that the assembly hall resembles a forest of ears. – What is this, I have been riding and riding, and haven't yet reached the meeting hall?

He looked out of the window and asked the young men, "Where are you taking me?" They replied, "We are taking you to where you were invited." Again he wrapped himself in clouds of smoke and looked at that forest of ears. As he looked the ears began to rattle against each other, as if they were applauding in honor of public speakers.

The car stopped and the young men helped Mr. Schreiholz to get out. Furious, Mr. Schreiholz yelled out, "Where am I?" "Have no fear, sir," the young men answered. "This is a populated neighborhood, and decent people live here, except that officials and leaders who have appointed themselves as city fathers have caused all this ruin. They spend so much of their time abroad taking good care of themselves that they have no time to take care of the city." "Who are you?" asked Mr. Schreiholz, his whole body breaking out in perspiration. "Calm yourself, Mr. Schreiholz." "Why do you seek to do me harm?" "God forbid," they replied, "far be it from us to seek to harm anyone. However, many misfortunes afflict the State, and we have no doubt that most of them are a result of our spending most of our time in making speeches, and thus we never get to any action. And since we are unable to take the people's attention away from the orators, we seek to take the orators away from the people, so that people's minds may be freed to think about themselves and how they spend their days and years. And if we were not completely disillusioned by the speakers and the orators, we would say that they too will profit from this, because, if they get into the habit of sitting down in silence, they will no longer feel within themselves that emptiness that desolates their hearts between speeches."

When Schreiholz saw that he had fallen into the hands of difficult people who treat public speakers with contempt, he controlled his anger and asked, "How long do you intend to keep me here?" "Until the audience will get tired of sitting and return home," they replied. "But suppose in the meantime they find another speaker to replace me?" asked Mr. Schreiholz. With a sigh the young men answered: "That did not occur to us. This is a most serious calamity, since for each and every speaker a hundred others can be found." As Mr. Schreiholz was biting his lips the young men invited him to enter. "Where to?" he asked. "Into this house, or perhaps into the house of another of our friends. Which is your choice?" "Which is my choice?" Mr. Schreiholz yelled with all his strength, "my choice is that fire come down from heaven and consume all three of you as one!"

One of them sighed and said, "We really deserve this for using strong-arm methods, but we rely on the mercies of heaven to have pity upon us, inasmuch as we have no alternative." Mr. Schreiholz looked at the young man disdainfully and said: "Do you really believe anything exists up there in heaven?" "Anyway," the young man replied, "here on earth nothing exists except speeches and orations, orations and speeches. And this, Mr. Schreiholz, is not good, not good Mr. Schreiholz, not good."

Mr. Schreiholz then inquired of the young men, "What, for example, do you wish for the country?" With a sigh the young men replied: "How should we know? It will take seven years before the hot air of the speech makers can be cleared out of one's brain so as to bring it back to normal. Only then may it be possible to think of anything." "I see that you are stronger than I," said Mr. Schreiholz. "Do with me what you will, but I want you to know that I will take my vengeance upon you." "We are not strong," said the young men sighing, "and as to vengeance, what vengeance can be visited upon us that we have not already suffered? You can see, sir, the extent of our desperation in the fact that we have even been led to act like kidnappers. Not only that, but we are worse than kidnappers, since they commit their crime for the sake of earnings, and we on the other hand take money out of our earnings to spend on renting a car. Well now, Mr. Schreiholz, where would you like us to take you?"

"Is there a coffee house around here?" Mr. Schreiholz inquired. "No," they replied, there is no coffee house here. And if a man wants to pass away a leisurely hour what does he do?" They answered: "The people here are busy earning their livelihood, and don't have an hour of leisure for themselves." "And what do they do on Sabbaths and holidays?" "Those who are learned sit and study, and those who are not learned learn from those who are learned." "Well," observed Mr. Schreiholz with a smile, "each to his own pleasure." "Yes, each to his own pleasure," the young men replied. But they did not smile because they envied those to whom it was given to enjoy this pleasure.

Mr. Schreiholz accompanied the young men to a room in which a small lamp was the only source of light. The room was small and contained plain wooden furniture. This was the kind of room and the kind of furniture Mr. Schreiholz knew in his childhood. The clothes he had worn in his childhood days also resembled the clothes worn by the three young men, inasmuch as Mr. Schreiholz, as most of his colleagues, was not born in a princely palace and did not wear princely clothes in his childhood. But since his elevation in public life he felt obliged to pamper his body with fine clothes and a fine home. He turned his attention away from the room and all that the room reminded him of and asked, "Do you have a newspaper?" "We have no newspaper here," his host replied, "but if it is a book you want, that you can find here." "And what is this?" Mr. Schreiholz asked. "This is a page from a newspaper in which the grocer wrapped the loaf of bread which I bought," answered his host. Mr. Schreiholz spread out the newspaper page and what he saw both pleased him and made him sigh. He was pleased because he saw his name and the public notice of the meeting which he was to have addressed. And he sighed because he had been prevented from speaking. After he finished reading the page he asked to have the radio switched on, but was told that they had no radio. "No coffee house, no radio – how do you live?" asked Mr. Schreiholz. They replied: "While others pass away their days and years in the coffee house or listening to the radio, we live our lives according to the will and desire of our Creator."

Mr. Schreiholz looked at his watch and asked, "Well my friends, how long are we going to remain here?" "Only a little while longer Mr. Schreiholz," they said. He again looked around back and forth. The small room put him in a good mood, similar to the mood he had often experienced before he became public property. He recalled the days when he sat and read and studied by the light of a small lamp. Alas, days that are past and gone, after which came noisy and turbulent days. How did this happen? After he filled his mind full of books he was tempted to speak in public. The first speech he made did not come off well, because his mind was still full. As his mind began to be emptied his speeches improved.

As he sat and thought he looked at these young men whose humility and poverty reminded him of himself when he was a young man. He took a new cigar, trimmed it, and placed it in his mouth. He lit it and began to blow smoke. His lips curled upward, and his paunch began to shake as a paunch that is filled with laughter. He put down his cigar, looked at those around him, and said, "I want to make a deal with you."

"A deal?" asked the young men in bewilderment. "After all, we are not businessmen, and we are not familiar with business dealings." "Listen to me first and then you will reply," said Mr. Schreiholz. "Next week my friend Walzer is to be the speaker. You know that windbag. If you do to him what you have done to me I shall forgive you and will lodge no complaint against you." The young men laughed and said, "Sounds like a good idea, but…" "But you are poor people," echoed Mr. Schreiholz, "and you have no extra money for renting a car each week. If you had the money would you do it? However, I have one condition before you agree to do it. The week after next another of my friends is scheduled to speak." The young men uttered a loud and troubled sigh. Mr. Schreiholz laughed, took but his wallet, and said, "Here is enough money to rent two or three cars. Will you shake hands on it now?" Each shook his hand and said, "It will be done!"

A sense of joy overcame dear Mr. Schreiholz so that he forgot where he was. And if the young men did not have to rise early in the morning to go to work, he would have sat there talking with them until the next day or perhaps even the day after. For Mr. Schreiholz was blessed by a special gift, when he was not speaking in public he talked with anyone who happened to be around, so that his ears would not have to listen to what his heart says.

Not all mouths are the same. Mr. Lipman Schreiholz, the admired leader, loves to talk, whereas these young men love silence. One of them left the room to go bring a car to take Mr. Schreiholz to his home. Mr. Schreiholz noticed this and said, "Better use the cost of this car for one of my friends who is scheduled to speak in the future, and I will walk home." The young men agreed, walked with him half way to his house, and parted from him with great esteem. He too parted from them very affectionately.

Now let us look carefully and attentively at what followed. What Mr. Schreiholz had done to his colleagues they did to their colleagues, and their colleagues in turn, to their own colleagues, for most human beings do nothing original, but only imitate the deeds of others. As a result people began staying away from the assembly hall, because they had come numerous times but no speakers showed up. And since they did not go to hear speeches they stayed home. And since they stayed home some looked into a book, or took care of their children. And though the world has not yet changed for the good, a slight improvement is already beginning to be evident. For, since people do not spend their days and years listening to speeches, they turn their attention to bettering some of their ways. And since they better some of their ways, the State also is gradually improved.

– Translated by Isaac Frank

Peace Everlasting

I

THE STATE WAS IN GREAT TROUBLE. There had been no trouble like it since the day when the State was founded. The heavens did not send down rain, and the earth did not yield its produce. It was as if heaven and earth had vowed to make an end of the surviving remnant. The supply of food decreased and the number of bodies swollen with hunger increased. A grain of wheat was going for gold, and barley for silver. Milk had turned to water, and there was no water. For the Lord had not sent rain upon the earth.

Every day the sun rises in the sky like a flaming ball, to play with its populated earth, and every night the dry moon shines. As the heavenly hosts on high, so the hoarders of food on earth – their bellies bulged like cannon balls. The strong became weak, the weak became sickly from hunger, and the sickly shriveled and died.

Troubles never come singly. When all strength had failed, a rumor was heard that enemies surrounded the State. The enemy had not yet entered the State, but he was very near. Even in normal times the State imports food; now that the State was surrounded by enemies neither food nor drink could enter. The citizens should have taken up arms, to fight, but the famine had weakened them. Everyone was weak, except the food hoarders, who were gaining strength each day, for the food hoarders created the impression that the country needed them since they labor for the public good, supervising the food supply, and if you trouble them with fighting, the entire country would be dying of hunger.

The enemy, seeing that there was no one who would stand against him, drew nearer, he from without and the famine from within. We thought that the trouble had already reached its peak, but an even greater trouble appeared, for the storehouse of trouble is bottomless, and there is no trouble which is not surpassed by another.

The State should have anticipated calamity with counsel. But the citizens of the State are divided into two sects, the covered-heads and the bared-heads, and whatever one sect tries the other foils. Even each of the sects is split within itself, one faction hating the other, perhaps more than the enemy hates the covered-heads and the bared-heads put together.

How can one State be split, like two contending nations? This can be explained by the nation's history, which still exerts an influence, even though the world has changed and the nation's way of life has changed, and its youth has abandoned everything which was precious to their fathers.

This country has a tradition that its founding fathers were Jews, and of course it is customary for Jews to cover their heads, so some of them cover their heads. But why do some of them bare their heads? They consider themselves in the category of Jews who lived before the time of Revelation, who had not yet been commanded to cover the head; therefore they bare their heads. And since one group covers the head and the other group bares the head, they are split, and they hate each other. But why should covered-heads hate each other, since all of them over the head? Well, some wear skullcaps and others wear hats, some wear square skullcaps and others round skullcaps, some are as large as a house and others smaller than a louse, some are of rags and others of silk. And one does not need a head especially – just so long as it is covered. And why should bared-heads hate each other, since all of them bare the head? Well, some of them have wavy hair and others cut it short, some are bald and others have a high forehead. And one does not need a head especially – just so long as it is bare.

As their heads differ, so do their opinions. One sect nods to the East; the other sect nods to the West. The only reason that they ever nod at each other is to ram their skulls together. Therefore, they do not join in debate over matters of state. They agree on one thing only: Each sect maintains that all the evils which befall the country are due only to its opponent, and if this author had no qualms about writing superfluous statements he would declare that both sides speak the truth.

II

There was in that State one man who belonged neither to the covered-heads nor to the bared-heads. He was just a man. If he had to be classified he would bare his head; otherwise he would not. He saw that a national disaster seemed inescapable. He said, "I will pray for rain, before the entire country dies of starvation." This should always come first – pleading to the Merciful One for mercy – but it had been forgotten by the citizenry, for it is human nature to forget what we should remember. He went to every synagogue and study hall in the State, but did not find a place for his prayer, since all of the country's covered heads were assembled at them for their conferences. Garbed in sack-cloth and ashes, he went out to a field, a place where no one lives, for the State's citizens usually spend all their days in the city, where one can listen to speeches and the like. That man prostrated himself in prayer and in supplication before the Holy One Praised Be He, and pleaded for rain to fructify the desolate earth, that its children would not die of starvation.

The Holy One Praised Be He had been anticipating the prayers of the citizens, for He is a God who desires lovingkindness and wishes His creatures well. Now, to allow them to eat their bread with a clear conscience, He ordained the order of prayer, so that they should first pray and then be rewarded, just as a cantor takes payment for his prayer from the sexton. However, since the citizens of the country were preoccupied with arguments and debates, they did not have time to remember their Creator, who redeems and saves, and is merciful in all times of trouble and distress, and who has it in His power to benefit His creatures if they are deserving of deliverance and mercy.

So they did not remember what they should remember – until people heard that one man had pleaded for rain.

Reports reached the leaders of the country and they were alarmed, covered-heads and bared-heads alike. The bared-heads were alarmed, lest he be answered from heaven and they be found knowing there is something above them. The covered-heads were alarmed, asking: Is it possible that a man who had not studied in their yeshiva, and who was not counted among the learned sages, who is not a disciple of their Rebbe, is it possible that he stuck his nose into their business? For when it comes to prayer, who is accepted in the Presence of He who hears prayer, if not they? All of the sects began moaning and groaning, each sect for a different reason, but all for the same basic reason that this man who had prayed for rain was with neither one nor the other of them. And since they all were moaning the distance between their opinions decreased, in theory if not in practice. However, the newspapers, may they be recalled with good thoughts, are of great value in leading theory along into practice. One small question was asked in the newspapers: This man – who sent him? In whose name had he been received in God's Presence? They began making disagreeable remarks about a little man who cloaks himself in greatness, and they were complaining that God had left the great men of the State, to become attached to a little man who belongs to no party. And once an opening had been made for talkers, all thinkers in the country came out to disclose their opinion that that act was liable to destroy the very foundations of the country, not to mention law and order, for anyone without authorization from the community who sets himself up as a representative can be considered as one of the dissolute criminals who respect nothing, destructive of the State's basic law.

All the ink spilled by the pens was absorbed bodily. The entire country began coughing up such things, until nobody could say anything that had not already been said by his comrade. The two of them would be astonished, for they had been opponents through the years, but now they are of one opinion, and not only is their opinion the same but their speech as well, even their tongues, which utter those things in the same way that the other sought to say them.

They decided to send deputations and delegations to the country's leaders. The leaders welcomed them and put themselves at their disposal, to wage defensive and offensive war with that one who had violated the national law and order. But words were still as far from actions as actions are from words. And were it not for the hoarders of food, they would have fulfilled their obligations through words, and words upon words.

The hoarders of food, covered-heads and bared-heads alike, since they are preoccupied with one matter, that is money, all of their days, have taught themselves to forego everything other than money, for money can smooth over opinions and win the hearts of others, like a bank note which one cashes, or like one penny added to another. All the moneyed men in the country gathered for formal consultation concerning the lawlessness of the generation which breaks the law and seeks to uproot all foundations of discipline, in this difficult hour when the nation is depressed, downcast, stricken and suffering, and everyone in the country is hungry, and it is well known that in the end hungry men, since they have nothing to lose, could easily revolt. And here the author must state that the food hoarders speak words of truth. The citizens of the country were so hungry and weak that the very shoulders which bore food and drink to the hoarders' banquets were bending and drooping beneath their burden.

Wine accomplishes a great deal; good food accomplishes a great deal. And when the belly is full, the body is satisfied; and when the body is satisfied, the mind is clear. All the food hoarders began seeing each other as of one mind. Immediately they were gracious to one another and greeted one another warmly. Due to the great amounts which the covered-heads ate and drank, they were sweating and fanning themselves with their skullcaps; as a result, their heads were bared. Similarly, due to the great amounts which the bared-heads ate and drank, their heads were covered with sweat, and whenever they would wipe them with handkerchiefs their heads would be covered. Each group was surprised at itself, surprised at what it had said about its opponent, when they were alike in every respect. And when they realized that they really were equals they reached an agreement to do something equally appropriate for them all. What that something was we soon shall see.

Something which at first appeared to be supernatural began happening quite naturally. How so? All of the country's hoarders of food began inciting and arousing the great men of the country, the covered-heads covered heads, and the bared-heads bared heads, until all of them gathered at a place called Lippery, for everyone whose lips serve him well can master the citizens of the country through speechmaking. They began discussing in earnest what to do, lest on the morrow rain should fall, and the earth yield its produce and all law and order would be overcome, since the rain would not be falling because the heads of state agreed that the country needed rain but because of that man who had gone off by himself to pray for rain. And this affair was likely to bring destruction and annihilation in its wake, for any person at all could then do whatever his heart desires without the agreement of the nation's leaders. And since the deeds of the Holy One Praised Be He come when least thought of, and the rains could come suddenly, they all agreed unanimously to accept whatever suggestion would be made first, without debates and postponements, without changes and delays.

So all the great men of the State were gathered as one to discuss the matter formally. There were bared-heads, whose heads have made no peace with either the sun or the rain, since the one dries out their brains and the other drips on their bald pates glistening at the heavens, and who were occupied all their days with making barriers between themselves and the sky. They spread a type of tent over themselves during the summer because of the sun, and during the winter because of the rain. And since all their thoughts are concentrated upon matters separating them from the heavens, they were first with a proposal, suggesting that a rain shelter be made, to stretch from one end of the State to the other, so that even if the Master of rain caused rain to fall to fructify the earth, the rain nevertheless would not reach the earth and would not cause it to bring forth anything, and law and order in the land would be maintained, and the deeds of that one who sought to overturn law and order and of those who rose to assist him would be null and void. The covered-heads, who think only of covering things over, considered the suggestion, and accepted it happily.

Immediately thereafter they gathered for a second meeting and appointed measurers for the entire State, to measure the length and width of the land, and they selected a committee to gather all the country's weavers, to weave a carpet the size of the State. They selected another committee to gather all of the country's carpenters, to make poles from which the carpet would be hung. They selected another committee to determine the location of the poles. Another committee which they selected was a committee of forcers who know how to give advice on how to force poles into the ground. They selected another committee to supervise the workers. And then they made just an ordinary committee, which was divided into two sections, ordinary committee A and ordinary committee B. After all the committees had been appointed, they appointed a committee of all the committees.

After all these committees had been selected, a special committee was selected to name the carpet, for everything which has a name becomes a slogan and is likely to make money. And money was certainly needed for the manufacture of the carpet and the construction of the poles and especially for the support of the committees. All members of the committee gathered together for a meeting. They finally decided to give the naming into the hands of the Society Linguistia, the Linguistia being in charge of all linguistic matters, all of whose members are linguists and verbally verbal, expert in all languages, among them even members who are expert in the language of our State.

All of the members gathered together and rented large buildings where they installed secretaries and aides, and sat down to consider names. There were some who suggested the carpet be called Preventerific, since it was to prevent the rain from touching the ground, and some suggested it be called Enablerific, since it would enable the country to maintain law and order. And there were those who suggested the carpet be named Coverific, since it was to be a cover. And some suggested it be named Protesterific. They finally decided to name it Protesterific, since it involved a protest, the basic purpose of making the carpet being to protest against the rain which was likely to ruin all law and order in the country. And why did all the names end with the letters "erific"? Because poetry was on the decrease while poets were on the increase, and the linguists had seen fit to aid them by making their rhymes easier for them. Immediately they appointed two committees: one to decide whether to write Protesterific all in capital letters or all in lower case letters, and one to decide whether to write it all in lower case letters or all in capital letters. A third committee was appointed to decide whether to spell it Protesterrific, with three r's, or Protesterific, with two r's, since the citizenry was still split over every letter, some preferring one spelling and others another spelling. It came to the point where each and every letter was like two kinds of letters. Finally they determined to write it with both a capital letter and lower case letters, in order to show respect for the proponents of both positions.

Once the carpet had a name, all of the country's speakers began speaking about law and order and about Protesterrific, and all of the newspapers were publishing their speeches, in addition to the articles which the journalists themselves were writing. Even the poets were not out of action, but knocked out their verses with great satisfaction; indeed whose mind dare we encumber just to remember all of their number, for their very sound the ends of the earth did rankle, and all the frogs of Egypt would not reach their ankle.

The great men of the country did not lose sight of the major principle. They launched a drive for funds and appointed cashiers and collectors, salesmen and solicitors, and they too went out to every town and village, and organized meetings and spoke. They began by attacking the breakers of law and order and ended by praising the Protesterrific, which unites the entire country and leads to peace. Hearts waxed enthusiastic and all hands were warmed. From holes and cracks the farmers brought out seed which they had hidden in order to sow their fields, and they made large banquets for the nation's select who had brought peace and unity. While they were eating and drinking, brides and bridegrooms came, these bringing dowries and those their bridal veils. Before there was time to congratulate them, old men and women came with the burial shrouds they had prepared for themselves. And if anyone did not bring anything he was persecuted until he gave in spite of himself.

They collected the donations and the contributions, and brought in weavers and carpenters. The weavers made the carpet and the carpenters the poles, each craftsman using the characteristic color of his group, black coloring black, red red, and blue blue. The work on the carpet was completed and the work on the poles was finished. They hung the carpet on the poles and spread it out from one end of the country to the other. The citizens gaze at the carpet and rejoice at the Protesterrific and say, what a lovely Protesterrific, what a lovely Protesterrific. Lawless men have sought to destroy all discipline but our eyes are upon the Protesterrific; happy are we who have been privileged to see the restoration of discipline to its rightful place, and the unity of the nation.

III

The prayer of that man accomplished a little, and the will of the Holy One Praised Be He accomplished everything. The Holy One Praised Be He produced the key for rain to open His good treasury, the heavens. The key, which had not been used for many years, had become rusty. And when the key was stuck into the sky, an enormous noise was heard, the sound of thunder before the rain. And from that rust the heavens were blackened, and were filled with clouds. And after the noise, rain began falling. The carpet split into shreds. The rain reached the earth and saturated the ground. For it is the way of the citizenry to do their deeds haphazardly, since the idea, not the deed, is the main thing. And so rain fell, to slap at the face of every man. The colors of the carpet blurred; the black became red and the red became blue and the blue became black, or red, until it was impossible to tell the difference between black and red or between red and blue.

This author often has the opportunity to teach that there is no evil unaccompanied by goodness, and he still maintains this outlook, and has no fear of mockers. However, just as there is no evil unaccompanied by goodness, so there is no goodness unaccompanied by evil since, in this world, goodness and evil are intermingled, and everything good for this one is bad for that one. Since a great deal of rain did fall, causing the earth to yield its produce, bread to eat and water to drink, the hungry were happy but the sated were sad, since the prices of all the food which they had hoarded went down and they suffered losses. And even the happiness of the great men of the country was incomplete: the covered-heads, for their skullcaps and hats had been mangled, and the bared-heads, for the rain had slapped at their bald pates.

Having described how the State was delivered from its domestic enemy, we are obliged to tell how the foreign enemy besieged the State to make war. But now is not the time to talk of such things, since we are tasked with fighting obligatory wars against our enemy.

— Translated by Jules Harlow

The Orange Peel

An orange peel littered the public domain. One of those peels whose twin you might find on any street or any corner. Everyone who passed by the peel stumbled over it. The persnickety checked their shoes to make sure they hadn't been dirtied, the unpersnickety scraped their feet and walked on, for even a person with eyes on the back of his head can't keep track of every peel littering the sidewalk. The peel lay there, and every passer-by stumbled over it. One old man slipped and fell, gathered his bones, and got up. The same happened to a girl. Her bones didn't scatter, but the contents of her purse did: a mirror and a comb, a shining row of pins, puffs, powders, patches, billet-doux, some love letters from her friend's husband, and various trappings for the beautification of body and spirit. Being young and not unlovely, all ran to her aid and gathered the dispersed. The orange peel, having nothing to do with the contents of her purse, stayed where it was.

Grouches and grumblers who spend their lives feeling sorry for themselves saw the peel and envied it, for it lay there tranquilly, offending all and caring none. This envy gave way to anger, and they began to fume and rage at the callous well-offs and the poor peel. But the more level-headed residents of the State, ruled by logic and not by passion, looked kindly upon the peel. "The peel is not at fault," they said, "but who is? He who threw the peel. That glutton, gobbling up oranges and tossing their peels away and endangering the general public." Others, who were less concerned with philosophizing than with matters of State, and who never missed a chance to denounce its actions, said: "The litterer is not at fault, but who is? The City Council, who fails to send its workers to sweep up the peel. All *he* did was eat an orange – not foreign produce mind you, but a fruit of the Land – if only there were more like him, who are satisfied with what the State provides, and don't go about pining for imported fruits that cost a pretty penny. But the City Council, who fails to dispose of the peel – they deserve a telling off! What do we get for our taxes? We get fruit peels, that's what! The State collects taxes, but that's about it!"

One member of the crowd said, "Upon my soul, if that tax collector comes around, I'll slam the door in his face. We're better off using that tax money for health insurance, so that we won't end up like that old man who stumbled over the peel and slipped and fell."

A propagandist of the National Fund latched on to him and said, "Perhaps the good sir would be interested in investing his money in the National Fund, which purchases land and leaves it empty, with no chance of any peels, and no fear of slipping and falling."

The avowed tax evader fumed and replied, "They never fail to mention the National Fund! Never a day goes by without an appeal from the National Fund! Tu BiShvat was National Fund Day, and so was the Ninth of Av and Passover and every other day! Lord Almighty, couldn't You have created just one day when they *don't* ask for money? There are more days when they ask for money than days of the year!"

- "And the good sir gives?"
- "Do I have any choice but to give?"
- "And how much does he give?"
- "How much do I give? A pretty penny printed with the letters of the State. But please, Mister, what does the National Fund have to do with anything? If I'm not mistaken, we're talking about peels here!"

"Dear me," a State official's wife cried, "my mother-in-law broke her leg on a peel just like this. She was walking somewhere and she stumbled upon an orange peel – or a grapefruit peel or a banana peel or the devil knows what peel – and she slipped and fell and broke her right leg – or was it her left leg? She spent so much time lying in bed that she ruined seven sheets. And do you think that I was any better off when she finally recovered? The way she shuffled around the house and wagged her walking stick, I took off and fled abroad. I hadn't been abroad since the last Congress." Mention of the Congress proved quite the diversion.

The peel lay there still, blackening and shriveling and losing all its fruity glory. But that peel was more fortunate than most of its peers, who had been lying in the rubbish heap since the days of the last Congress, with no one giving them any thought. A certain linguist lived in the State, a real pedant, and he would keep track of the talk of the town and correct their mistakes of spelling, grammar, and pronunciation. He saw the peel and sought to set things right. He seized a passerby and said to him, "What have you to say about this peel?"

- "What is there to say, it's a peel like any other," he replied.

- "That's not what I meant," he said, "I'm not asking about the peel, I'm asking about its spelling. For years I've been crying that peel shouldn't be spelled with a double e. Yet the world insists on doing so, and it's an error we ought to rend our garments over."

For a moment it seemed that the peel itself would be forgotten for the sake of its spelling. As we said, however, it was a most fortunate peel, and before long it was once again the talk of the town. Very soon, another passerby passed by and saw the peel, remarking to the bystanders, "I wonder that no one's taken a picture of the peel and sent it to the papers. But we ought to first ask the movers and shakers to appeal to the writers to stir the people to fund the photos, so that all will be warned of the peril that threatens the passersby. And the Diaspora shouldn't be tightfisted either, so we need the pictures to be taken by a professional so that our brothers in the Diaspora can feast their eyes upon the sights of the Land."

Another stood by and said, "What's so offensive about this peel? On the contrary, it's a sign of freedom, that anyone in the State can act as he pleases, being upon his own turf." Another stood by and said to the person who sought freedom in the garbage, "What can we do? It says in the Talmud that Jerusalem should not be turned into a rubbish heap."

Another old man happened by, and said to him, "Have you observed everything in the Talmud except for that? Leave the Talmud to the observant. You bare-headed folk, isn't it enough that you've already taken the Bible – now you start eyeing the Talmud as well?"

The author of the Book of the State, fearing a quarrel, decided to get rid of the peel that was awakening such malice and envy. He picked up the peel and placed it where he placed it. A woman saw him and said, "And what of the other peels, and what of the other bits of paper and newspaper and all sorts of rubbish that litters the city? If you don't mind, Mister, there's an apple peel, and there's a grapefruit peel, and there's a tattered book, some scrap of missionary propaganda, all waiting to trip up some poor passerby, and there's a broken trap with a dead mouse, don't let them just lie there and stink up the air!"

Another person heard her. "Relax, lady," he said, "soon the Land'll be divided up, and no one yet knows if this place'll be ours or our enemy's, so what do you care if the rubbish stays there?" At the mere mention of partition, everyone pounced on him and began to argue. "What do you want from me?" he yelled, "I didn't say I'm in favor of partition, I only said what's in the papers!" And they screamed back.

The author of the Book of the State said to himself, "Partition or no partition, so long as we're here, I want our Land free of litter." He reached down and began clearing the mess.

As soon as he began cleaning, everyone began to shower him with advice, some helpful and some less so – how to scrape off the peels, how to clear them, where to put them, and so on and so forth. He was even aided by the heavens – that is, at that moment, the wind blew all the rubbish into the street. Pages of newspaper and old books of more sublime nature than fruit peels were lifted out of the bins and flapped against the faces of passersby. However, as their substance far outweighed their spirit, they lay themselves back in the garbage. The author of the Book of the State resumed his task, and his advisors resumed their task. There was enough advice to supply a large country.

Not all advice is equal, however. The author of the Book of the State picked up an orange peel, and someone advised him to get rid of a grapefruit peel first. He lifted up the grapefruit peel, and another told him that he ought to deal with that banana peel. He picked up the banana peel, and another advisor urged him to pick up that other peel first. To honor all opinions, the author of the Book of the State began using both hands at once. Unfortunately, people's advice far outnumbered the number of hands at his disposal. As he attempted to do everyone's bidding, his advisors began to bicker over what should be picked up first, and their arguments erupted into full scale fights.

Here, the author of the Book of the State must take note of an extraordinary incident. The State is often witness to her children squabbling with nary a policeman appearing to intervene, but at that very moment a policeman actually materialized and began to scold the crowd who raised a commotion in the public square. When the crowd realized that the policeman was not too pleased, they scattered and went on their way. When the author of the Book of State saw them disperse, he said to himself, "Now no one will hold me back from my task." Twice as fast, he cleared and gathered, until the street began to be purged of its filth.

The policeman saw the author of the Book of the State alone in the street and called to him, "Are you the one who caused all that commotion?" He took out his ticket book and wrote down his name to charge him for stirring the masses and disturbing the peace.

"Please, sir," said the author of the Book of the State, "allow me to explain what happened. As I was walking down the street, I saw an orange peel littering the public domain, waiting to trip up passersby, and no one was clearing it, so I said to myself, I'll go and clear it, and once I started I thought I might as well continue down the entire street."

"If so," said the policeman, pursing his lips, "then you admit that you were clearing the rubbish."

"Certainly," said the author, "nothing to deny, I told things as they are and I'm willing to repeat them."

"Well then," said the policeman, "where's your garbage collector's license?"

Once again, he took out his ticket book and heaped accusation upon accusation upon me, charging me for garbage collecting without a license. Just then, however, he recalled lunchtime, of blessed memory, and was most anxious to lunch, so he left without taking me into custody. The author of the Book of the State was left standing amidst the rubbish and said to himself, "Woe to he who tries to clear a bit of rubbish in this State, and woe to the State, who has yet to be cleared of its filth."

— *Translated by Sara Daniel*

On Taxes

Once again, the state was in need of money when there was none to be found, not even to pay the State clerks who always make sure to take their salaries in advance. Now, the State wasn't even able to pay what was overdue, and there was fear that they would declare a strike, as the schoolteachers often did, and the State would be left without its clerks.

The scoffers scoffed. "What shall they strike against," they leered, "against doing nothing, or against sitting around with their arms crossed? The ones to really pity are the coffee and bagel vendors in the government offices, whose livelihood depends on the clerks' coffee and bagel consumption. If the clerks strike, then the coffee and bagel vendors are in jeopardy."

But every reasonable person, who thinks before he scoffs, was concerned that if the State clerks would strike, then the State would collapse into chaos.

The State leaders and delegates of the people held an emergency meeting in the Chamber of Lippery, that is, the Cabinet, where all State issues are truncated. They hemmed and hawed and reached the conclusion that something must be done. Not just anything, but really something. Not a soul rose from his seat until the majority agreed to assemble a committee of experts to examine the situation.

They assembled a committee of the best of the State's economists, and added the best of the State's statisticians. Someone's house was confiscated for the committee's needs, and they held a meeting and investigated every last detail. Before very long they determined that the State owed a month's salary to its officials, and presented their findings together with a bill for the committee's expenditures.

The committee's conclusions caused uproar. Accusations and letters to the papers plunged the State into a state of turmoil. Some demanded to know why the State was withholding the clerks' salaries; others demanded that the committee's findings be examined by a legal committee and a committee of traders and manufacturers. These demands were supported by the people's representatives, the entire Chamber of Lippery, in order to gratify their constituents.

A committee of lawyers and one of traders and manufacturers were duly assembled. Both held meeting after meeting, examining the finer points of the matter in great depth. The lawyers, who based their research on the legal codes, determined that if the clerks failed to receive their salary, they were entitled to sue for payment, regardless of whether the employer in question was an individual or a collective; and if the judge determined that the law was on the side of the employer, then the employee would be required to pay what was due, excepting legal and judicial fees. The parallel committee reached similar conclusions, save that their experience with strikes led them to advise the State to pay, for if they failed to do so the clerks were liable to declare a strike, and then the State would be required to pay them for the duration of the strike, for as long as strikes were permitted by law, the State was liable to reach the state it now found itself in.

The State leaders saw the committee's conclusions and were in quite a state, for money was needed in order to pay the clerks, and no money was to be had in the State. The matter was reviewed once again and identical conclusions were reached, only there were no experts left to pin their hopes on.

"In your opinion," said the State leaders to the committee members, "the clerks must be paid, but payment requires money, and there is no money to be had. And we are unable to levy new taxes, as every national commodity – from thread to shoelace – is already taxed, and not a single commodity remains to be taxed."

"We realize the problem," replied the committee members to the State leaders, "but the task we were assigned was to analyze the issue, and we have analyzed the issue from every angle, and presented you with our conclusions, and we have nothing to add, except for this bill for the committee's expenditures for clerks and scribes and assistants and drivers, and here it is. Please see to it that the Reimbursement Committee pays promptly."

The State members who covet the fruit before planting the tree asked what would become of the State were its clerks to strike. The State scoffers scoffed, as was their wont, "Stay away from unnecessary expenditures, and cut back on cars and clerks and scribes and office aides and assistants." Some members of the State agreed and disagreed. They agreed that frugality ought to be implemented, but they were loath to cut back on the use of cars, for it was an honor for the State that its leaders travelled in special cars, rather than cram into buses, sinking into the mire and mud like everyone else. And in regard to the mire and mud that everyone sunk into, it ought to be investigated whether fixing the roads wouldn't threaten the livelihood of the shoe-shiners. And as for the matter of clerks and scribes and office aides and assistants, things ought to be left as they are, for to dismiss them would increase the idlers in the State, and they too would join the ranks of the State scoffers. In any case, they ought to make sure to use the telephone sparingly – if they invite their friends for an outing to a café or the like, they should have their assistants invite them rather than use the telephone, as every call costs the State such and such, and such and such tends to add up.

Everyone was still all a-hustle and a-bustle, and the clerks had already sent an ultimatum that they would strike if they weren't paid by such and such a day, and the State ought to pay them their due, if it were capable of doing so. And not only were the clerks set to strike, but their secretaries and scribes and aides and assistants, and assistants' assistants, had joined in their ultimatum.

As the State leaders saw that the matter would not suffer adjournment they resumed their discussion. Once again, they concluded that the matter ought to be investigated. They assembled a new committee. And as reason tends to remain consistent, that committee produced the same results as the previous committees, with the exception of their bill, which slightly exceeded that of their predecessors as the price of bread had since risen.

The committee's proposal that the clerks' salaries be paid was opposed by the Minister of Finance, who had received a report from the Treasury officials that not a penny was to be found in the State Treasury. The Chamber of Lippery, always ready to offer advice, demanded that a new committee interrogate the Chief Treasurer to cross examine the Treasury officials to determine precisely what was and what was not the content of the report that had been delivered to the Minister of Finance. This proposal was rejected by the majority, for everyone knows that underlings are far more informed than their superiors, as the real work is done by low-ranking clerks, and the higher one climbs up the ladder, the less actual information he is saddled with, so that he can concern himself with more pressing matters, such as cataloging all the jokes and witticisms in the State. As no alternate solution was proposed, however, the majority swallowed their objections and agreed to the assembly of a committee who would meet with the Chief Treasurer.

The committee was selected and met with the Treasurer. The Treasurer was a great collector of witticisms and knew that everyone knows how to tell a joke, and if someone doesn't, why, that in itself is funny. He was thrilled to meet with the committee, as if they were bringing a host of jokes with them. He also engaged them in some light banter, jovially and cordially, not missing a single joke about a single leader of the State. "Indeed," he said, "in all likelihood, the jokes that members of the State tell about them will probably immortalize them far more than their deeds, notwithstanding that their deeds are one long joke themselves. And he went on and on until the committee members remembered why they had come in the first place, and spoke up about it. In an instant his jovial mien darkened and his lips twisted and his snout puffed up and his earlobes reddened and he looked for all the world like any other State clerk. And if they hadn't known otherwise, no one would have guessed that he was capable of understanding a joke. He immediately let his chair tip back, stood up with grave solemnity and led them to the Treasury, whereupon he handed a silver key to the head of the committee. In these very words he said, "Whenever I open the vault with a bronze key, I find it empty, so I had a silver key made, in the hope that in honor of the new key, and in your honor, gentlemen, the vault will fill with silver. In any case, it couldn't hurt to whisper 'open sesame' first."

The committee members returned empty-handed, but full of jokes. The State leaders and the representatives of the people reexamined the possibility of levying new taxes. They investigated the matter and found that there was not a single commodity, or even half a commodity, that remained untaxed.

The representatives of the people in the Chamber of Lippery, who know that there is a season for all things, saw that election time was approaching, and wished to endear themselves to their voters by showing them honor. They proposed approaching the people, for who is as knowledgeable and wise as an entire nation? This proposal was unanimously accepted. The democrats agreed because of the proposal's democratic nature. The aristocrats agreed because they reassured themselves that the nation is only as good as its representatives, so the proposal is doomed to fail anyway.

The proclamation was issued across the country: whoever had a proposal was invited to come forth. And here the author of the Book of the State must add that it was unwise of the State leaders to approach the people, because once the nation as a whole is permitted to state its opinion, one never knows what it might occur to them to say. With the issue of the proclamation, the State fell under national scrutiny. Some suggested that a committee investigate whether there ought to be so many clerks in the first place, given that they are a national scourge; others added that the meetings and gatherings and conferences and feasts and celebrations that the State leaders hold in each other's honor are no less of a scourge. General complaints rose from the four corners of the State. As for the proposals themselves, the author of the Book of the State sees no value in mentioning them, considering their utter irrelevance for this world.

Once the State leaders realized that no good was to come from the people's suggestions; and, worse off, that their words were quite treacherous, they cancelled the proclamation and confiscated the papers that had published it. Once again, the government of the State was restored to the hands of its leaders.

The State leaders and leaders of leaders held an emergency meeting – back to routine. Whoever it was stood up and declared that whoever had made that proposal ought to be censured for bringing the State to the brink of disaster. His proposal was met with fierce opposition, as it was unclear precisely who ought to be censured, as the Chamber of Lippery had accepted it unanimously. They therefore went through the motions of censure without specifying who was being censured. They then readdressed their agenda, namely how to find the money to pay the clerks and their secretaries and scribes and assistants. In order to gain time they agreed to refer to one general question, namely, how to get money. They sat for as long as they sat and made speeches, the most notable being Mr. Schreiholz's sophisticated speech, which could, without exaggeration, be considered a national treasure. Mr. Walzer attempted to surpass him and did not succeed, and even if one might suggest that his attempt was unsuccessful because the audience was weary from Mr. Schreiholz's speech, which could hardly be considered brief – well, no one's could be considered brief. As the speakers made their speeches and the bickerers bickered, the ultimatum drew nearer, with not a penny to throw against the looming strike.

The State, however, is a fortunate State, rising to the occasion even in the face of doom. It so happened one day that an elderly member of the Chamber of Lippery forgot his walking stick at work. When he returned home and attempted to stand it in its place, he realized that in his absentmindedness he had forgotten it in the Chamber of Lippery. Though at first he was furious at the Chamber attendants for failing to hand it to him, he hadn't time to be furious for long, for his dinner was already on the table. And so he sat down to eat and deferred his anger to the next day. Yet between one spoonful and the next he could not stop thinking about his walking stick, and the more he thought the more he marveled how an old man like himself had managed to walk without it. The next day he told the story to the entire Chamber of Lippery. The older members were green with envy while the younger ones congratulated him and said that before long he would be growing new teeth to replace his false ones.

One member of the Chamber of Lippery, however, did not join in the banter because he was too busy thinking of how the matter might be put to State use. As soon as the Chamber convened he took the floor and declared, "Gentlemen, please give me your attention: I have a proposal to make!" Some of the Chamber members lent an ear; others sat and drew funny faces or already began planning their rebuttals. "I have the solution," announced the speaker, "and I must admit that it is perfect. Please, gentlemen, consider carefully before you answer: what is the one thing, my friends, that we have forgotten to tax? We have forgotten, my friends, to tax walking sticks. They alone remain public parasites that evade their civic duty. That, gentlemen, is why I propose to tax them just as we tax all useful implements. Are walking sticks to be more privileged than spectacles, on which we levy a tax? Are they more special than false teeth, which are taxed also? And if they are indeed more special, that only means that they deserve a special tax. In my humble opinion, gentlemen, the walking stick is a human accessory and should be taxed as such. That, my friends, is the substance of my remarks, to which I have nothing to add except to say that although the wisdom of my proposal is undebatable, I nevertheless table it for debate as is the custom of this house."

The Chamber of Lippery was so stunned by the proposal that no one could think of a thing to say against it. It was only when a motion was moved to thank its author that several disinterested voices objected that for the Chamber to thank a member of the Chamber was like a person thanking his own self, which was an absurdity so great that the motion should be struck down at once. And indeed it was, although it was agreed to enter it in the protocol together with the reason for its rejection. Then the proposed tax was thrown open to debate and the Chamber voted to appoint a committee of statisticians to determine how many walking sticks there were in the State. It also voted to form a committee of economists to decide how walking sticks should be assessed.

A third committee was chosen to establish whether crutches should be considered walking sticks also, and if so, whether they should be taxed as one stick or as two, and if as two, whether they should be taxed by the unit like the lenses of spectacles or by weight like false teeth. The crutch committee appointed a subcommittee to investigate the question of teachers' canes and decide if they should be taxed as work tools or luxury items, since there were teachers who thrashed their pupils bare-handed instead of caning them and others who kicked them with their feet. A fourth committee, composed of historians, physicists, and bota-nists, was appointed to investigate if walking sticks could indeed turn into serpents and almond branches as claimed by the Bible. Meanwhile, the tax committee established a commission of inquiry to determine if a walking stick that was temporarily a serpent or an almond branch should be taxed as a walking stick or not. These committees quickly reported back to the steering committee, which presented its conclusions to the finance committee, which forwarded them to the ways-and-means com-mittee, which found ways and means of putting them into practice. And so, employing its statutory powers, the State enacted a walking stick tax.

At first the new tax was accepted quite matter-of-factly, not only by those who didn't own walking sticks but also by those who did. Indeed, some walking stick owners were proud of the tax, which enabled them to boast that they went about with walking sticks less for their own personal convenience than as a contribution to the pub-lic welfare. In time, however, walking sticks grew rarer and rarer until they disappeared entirely. What did the cripples and old people do who could not get along without them? They used umbrellas instead to evade taxes. When the State saw that it was losing revenue, it passed a new law decreeing that possession of a walking stick was taxable whether the stick was used or not. It also rejected the appeal of the covered-headed citizens who sought to pay only six-sevenths the tax on the grounds that their religion forbade them to use walking sticks one day a week. It was no concern of the State, said the State, whether they used their walking sticks on the Sabbath or not, and it proceeded to hire a force of walking stick inspectors and another of special tax collectors.

It is only fair that the author of the Book of the State should praise the State's leaders at this point, for while there was much grumbling that the latter brooked no taxes that were to their own personal disadvantage, we can see that this was clearly not the case. Indeed, they not only passed the walking stick tax despite the fact that they were subject to it themselves, they even added an amendment requiring everyone to buy a walking stick whether he or she needed it or not. The walking stick owners took to walking with their sticks again, and there was now such a demand for them that the merchants all raised their prices. Whoever could afford one bought it and paid the tax, while whoever couldn't was exempt.

When the State saw that the merchants were diminishing the number of taxpayers, it established a committee of experts to establish price controls for walking sticks and added an amendment to the amendment making it a criminal offense to sell a walking stick for more than its legal price. What did the merchants do? They took their walking sticks off the racks and began selling them on the black market. What did the State do? It announced that it would import walking sticks from abroad. This measure so frightened the merchants that they resumed selling walking sticks over the counter and the price dropped so sharply that everyone could now afford one. Soon, however, there were no walking sticks left to buy. Moreover, some people started to grumble that although they owned thin walking sticks, they had to pay as much as did those who owned thick ones, while short citizens complained that they should be taxed less than tall ones, whose walking sticks were much longer.

One complaint led to another and before long the whole State was up in arms. The Chamber of Lippery was hastily convened and speeches were given in praise of both walking sticks and their taxes. Since the full texts of these speeches appeared in all the newspapers, there is no need to repeat them here. But we will mention the Chamber's decision, which was to send a lumber-purchasing mission abroad so that every citizen could have a walking stick. This step was necessary because the State did not have enough trees. And why didn't it? Because whenever a tree was planted it was uprooted by schoolchildren for their Tu BiShvat celebrations. A committee was appointed to negotiate an international bank loan for the purchase of the lumber, and another was set up to determine where the lumber should be bought.

The committee members approached the Head of the Union of Clerks and asked them to postpone the strike. The Head of the Union of Clerks, who was a genial fellow and well-known collector of nail clippers, warmly received the committee members, and even showed them his collection, which was an impressive display of nail clippers ranging from biblical times to nail trimmers such as those used by the State's very own clerks and secretaries. They sat and discussed the state of the State and its needs. During the conversation he disclosed that he was about to donate his entire collection – whose equal could not be found in any other state – to his own beloved country. When the committee members perceived that the Head Clerk's heart was merry, they began to persuade him to cancel the strike – after all, they were about to import trees to make into walking-sticks to sell in order to exact taxes to pay the clerks' salaries. The Head Clerk, who was a practical man, agreed to postpone the strike. Like the great ones who rose to fame for their great deeds, and had the custom of peppering their speech with philosophical sayings, he added, "Is it not written in the book of Solomon's Proverbs, 'A roasted pigeon for tomorrow's lunch is better than a house full of raven corpses,' meaning that the promise of payment is better than strikes and squabbles."

Nor did the other committees sit and do nothing; they travelled abroad and borrowed money, while others imported the thickest trees that had ever been seen in the State. Once the wood had arrived, however, there were no saw-wielders or axe-bearers to be found, as the State was used to importing its wares and there wasn't a single woodcutter left in the State. The State confiscated several lots from their owners, filled them with the wood, and appointed guards to protect them from thieves. The guards constructed little huts and sat and guarded. Impressed with the importance of guarding State property, they did not leave their stations for an instant, not even venturing home for a snack. When they had to eat, they cooked their food over fires made from the wood, and in the winter months, they made little bonfires to keep themselves warm. The bachelors were visited by their girls and the married men by their wives and children. Neighbors came to visit their neighbors, and the neighbors' neighbors followed suit. Little by little the wood was burned, until nothing remained but ashes. Passersby complained that the wind was blowing the ashes into their eyes and blinding them. When the State could no longer abide their grumbling, they appointed a committee to deal with the matter. The committee reached the conclusion that the ashes must be cleared, and they might be able to put it to good use, perhaps by selling it to scribes, for the preparation of ink. Their proposal, however, was rejected by the vendors of paper towels. When the committee saw that there was nothing to be done with the ashes but clear them, they consulted with the Geographic Society to find a suitable site to dump the ashes. The Geographic Society searched the entire State and determined that there was nowhere to be found, as every empty lot was reserved for conferences and official gatherings and celebrations. "There is, however," said the Geographic Society, "plenty of room in the sea, and perhaps that new corporation, Pride of the Sea, Inc., will allow the ashes to be dumped in the sea." Pride of the Sea, Inc., a new enterprise seeking State support, immediately placed itself at the State's disposal and said that they would be delighted to make room in the sea, but seeing as the ashes were on land and the sea is somewhat confined to its borders, someone would have to transport the ashes to the shore and Pride of the Sea, Inc., would load it onto their ships. The State issued a proclamation that every freight company in the State is requested to put forth a bid. The Cooperative Corporation for the Transportation of Ashes, Ltd., won the bidding and loaded the ashes onto camels and donkeys and mules and wagons and carts and horses and vehicles until the shore, whereupon Pride of the Sea, Inc., loaded their ships and cast the ashes into the sea. Not long passed before the ashes were cleared. Once the lots were empty their owners attempted to take back their property, but the guards denied them access, based on the principle of status quo. As this squabble is no concern of the State, neither is the author of the Book of the State concerned with it, and, rather than dwell upon the issue, he wishes to return to the matter at hand – namely, the matter of walking sticks.

As there were no woodcutters to be found in the State, more emissaries were sent abroad, this time to purchase regulation walking sticks of uniform shape, thickness and length, to prevent grumblers from grumbling that other sticks were longer or thicker or finer than theirs. This, of course, did not prevent the grumblers from grumbling that the State ought to have entrusted the task of importing walking sticks to wholesalers, who are accustomed to cutting costs, unlike the State agents, who habitually wasted State funds and never worked a day in their lives, and hadn't the foggiest notion of how hard a person had to work before he even saw a single cent.

Let us leave the grumblers and their grumbles aside and turn to State endeavors. Before very long the entire nation had managed to get hold of walking sticks and the State had managed to get hold of enough taxes to pay the clerks, down to the very last ones, who had been appointed to implement the taxation of walking sticks.

Ostensibly, the author of the Book of the State could now put down his pen, and trouble it no more, as the State affairs have been settled. The State offices are open and the clerks are once again serving the State, and the coffee and bagel vendors are once again brewing coffee and baking bagels. Yet the author of the Book of the State does not yet lay down his pen. Not because of the teacher strike or the neglect of Torah study, for even if the Torah were to be left to gather dust in the corner, it would still be the Torah. And not out of pity for the youth who know nothing of the Torah, for even in the best schools the youth are too busy for Torah study, as they are constantly being recruited for the needs of the State. For example, an entire nail clipper collection was just donated to the State, and now the students are being sent out to raise funds for the building of a museum. Rumor has it that the museum is to be of vast proportions, given the number of clippers from around the world that the State emissaries have collected for themselves and their peers.

If so, why is the author of the Book of the State unable to lay down his pen? For there are still matters that must be dealt with in the State, dealt with and made right, and the author of the Book of the State must write about them. And doubtlessly, things will sort themselves out, for the State is fortunate. Even peace, which transcends nature, has found its way to the State, as discussed in the above chapter, entitled "Peace Everlasting."

– Translated by Sara Daniel

Annotations to *Chapters from The Book of State*

128. Book of Judges sees the Benjaminites seizing women for wives / Judges 21.

129. Schreiholz / Lit. meaning of name "Screaming Tree." It has been speculated that Agnon modeled something of Mr. Schreiholz on Zalman Shazar (1889-1974), Israel's third president. Shazar (né Shneur Zalman Rubashov) was an activist in Zionist politics and later a member of the Knesset from the time of the founding of the State. He was an author and poet, and known as a flowery orator, a quality passed over to the character of Schreiholz. The character of Schreiholz also appears in Agnon's short story "The Letter," in *A Book That Was Lost: Thirty-Five Stories* (The Toby Press), pp. 485-514.

137. The heavens did not send down rain, and the earth did not yield its produce / Deuteronomy 11:17.

137. For the Lord had not sent rain upon the earth / Genesis 2:5.

138. Bare-heads before the time of Revelation / Prior to the giving of the Law at Sinai; that is, they were secular.

139. As their heads differ, so do their opinions / Cf. Berakhot 58b: "Our Rabbis taught: If one sees a crowd of Israelites, he says, 'Blessed is He who discerneth secrets,' for just as the faces of each differ, so do their opinions."

139. Eat their bread with a clear conscience / The Hebrew text makes reference to kabbalistic concept of *lehem di-kissufa* (lit. "bread of shame"), which is used to explain the need for prayer, explaining that all-powerful God, who could provide all at His will, still requires the Jew to pray for sustenance so as not to receive his needs provided for without an awareness of his own needs.

142. Lippery / The Hebrew text refers to a place called *Siftotayim*, a witty Agnonism to convey that this Parliament is a place of mere lip service, where speech-making, not action, is the focus. It has been alternatively translated as Tonguey (i.e., a place for wagging ones tongue), but we have unified the translation across these stories.

143. Society Linguistia / The Hebrew text mentions *Hevrah Leshoni-yah*, a clear reference to, and satire of, the Hebrew Language Committee (later the Academy of the Hebrew Language), founded in 1889 by Eliezer Ben-Yehudah, to advance the development and use of modern Hebrew amongst the Jewish population of Palestine. Although a member of the committee at one point, Agnon had a complicated relationship with the organization, and criticized certain aspects of its work.

145. An enormous noise / Ezekiel 3:12.

146. Obligatory wars / In halakhic literature (Sotah 44b, e.g.) obligatory wars of self-defense require all to go out in defense of the Jewish homeland, even a "bridegroom from under bridal canopy." In contrast, "optional wars" (*milhemet reshut*) can be initiated by the king with the assent of the Sanhedrin to expand the nation's borders. Agnon is ironically recasting the terms so that obligatory wars of self-defense (against foreign enemies) are now contrasted with the "optional wars" the Jewish people choose to fight among themselves, i.e., the topic of this story.

147. Pins... billet-doux / Sara Daniel points out the parallel to another great satire: Pope, *The Rape of the Lock* 1: 137-138.

148. National Fund / The Jewish National Fund was founded in 1901 to buy and develop land in Ottoman Palestine, later British Mandate for Palestine, and subsequently the State of Israel, for Jewish settlement.

148. Tu BiShvat / Fifteenth of the month of Shevat (usually falls late-January), a minor holiday on the Jewish calendar, also known as "The New Year of the Trees." In modern times the day became the focus of Zionist and pioneering activity, marked by the planting of trees.

149. Congress / The Zionist Congresses, initiated in Basel, Switzerland, in 1897, were yearly (or bi-yearly) conventions of the (World) Zionist Organization, first convened by Theodor Herzl.

149. Spelled with a double e / The translation captures something of the Hebrew original, which refers to a fashion (championed by the Language Committee) to favor "plene" spelling when not

adding vowel dots in modern Hebrew, thus the word *kelipah* (peel) is spelled including the Hebrew letter *yud*.

150. That Jerusalem should not be turned into a rubbish heap / Bava Kama 82b. The Talmud lists ten civic restrictions that were implemented in order to safeguard the sanctity of Jerusalem, not making garbage dumps within the city being one of them.

150. Already taken the Bible / Reference to secular Zionism's embrace of the Hebrew Bible (to the exclusion of its rabbinic interpretation trough the Oral Law) as a source of new Jewish identity and culture. This topic is discussed, most recently, in Ilana Pardes, *Agnon's Moonstruck Lovers* (University of Washington Press, 2013).

150. Land'll be divided up / A variety of "partition plans" had been floated to resolve Arab-Jewish tensions and competing claims to Palestine. This story having been written in 1939, Agnon could not yet have known of the ultimate decision by the United Nations General Assembly on November 29, 1947, to divide the British Mandate for Palestine into independent Arab and Jewish states.

153. On Taxes / The title, "*Al HaMissim*," is a word play on the holiday prayer "*Al HaNissim*" ("On the Miracles"), recited on Hanukkah and Purim.

155. From thread to shoelace / Genesis 14:23.

160. Turn into serpents and almond branches / References to the biblical miracles of Aaron's staff turning into a serpent in Pharaoh's court (Exodus 7:20) and its sprouting "buds, blossoms, and ripe almonds" (Numbers 17:8), as evidence of the exclusive right to the priesthood of the tribe of Levi during Korah's rebellion.

162. A roasted pigeon for tomorrow's lunch... / To highlight the character's pompous buffoonery, Agnon has placed this expression (decidedly not a verse from Proverbs) in the Head Clerk's mouth. Whether the adage itself is original to Agnon or an old Yiddishism remains unclear.

– Annotated by Jeffrey Saks

Introduction to
the Kaddish

Graves of the "Thirty Five" (*Lamed Heh*), Mount Herzl Military Cemetery, Jerusalem.

For Those Who Died in the Israeli Wars

A king of flesh and blood who goes out to war against his enemies
Brings forth his force to kill and to be killed.
There is doubt whether he loves his soldiers
Or whether he does not love his soldiers,
Whether they are important in his eyes
Or whether they are not important in his eyes.
And even if they are important in his eyes,
They are no more important than corpses,
Because the angel of death follows upon their heel to slay them.
And if one is struck down by a blade or a bullet
Or another means of destruction and killed,
Another is set in his place.
And the king ignores his loss.
For the nations of the world are great in number,
And their armies are great in number,
And if one of them is killed,
The king has many to replace him.

But our King,
The King of kings, the Holy One, blessed be He,
Desires life, loves peace and pursues peace,
Loves Israel His people and has chosen us from all the nations,
Not because we are greater in number,
For we are the least in number.
And because He loves us and we are few in number,

Each one of us is as important in His eyes as a whole regiment.
For He does not have many to set in our place.
Thus if one Jew dies (God forbid),
Distress falls upon the regiments of the King,
And a weakening comes to the kingdom of He who is blessed,
For His kingdom lacks one of its regiments
And the greatness of He who is blessed is lessened.

Therefore we pray after the death of each Jew.
Yitgadal ve-yitkadash shemah raba:
May the power of His Name be magnified,
And may no lessening of power come to Him
Who is blessed and sanctified
In the worlds He has created according to His will.
And let us not be in fear for ourselves
But for the glory of His holiness.
Ve-yamlikh malkhutah:
May it be revealed
And may you see His kingdom in its fullness, lacking nothing,
    God forbid.
*Be-ḥayeikhon uv-yomeikhon uv-ḥayai de-khol beit Yisrael bimherah
    uvi-zman kariv:*
If His kingdom is revealed in the world,
Then there is peace in the world
And blessing in the world
And song in the world
And much rejoicing in the world
And great consolation in the world
And the holy ones of Israel are beloved in the world
And His greatness continues to be magnified and expanded and
    not diminished *Le-olam.*

And if we pray thus for each one who dies,
How much the more so for our dear brothers and sisters
The children of Zion,
The slaughtered ones of the land of Israel,

Whose blood was spilled for the glory of His name
And for His people
And for His land
And for His inheritance.
Further,
Every dweller in the land of Israel is one of the company of the
    King of kings,
The Holy One blessed be He,
Whom the King has appointed as a guard of His palace.
If one of His company is killed,
He does not have others to set in his place.

Therefore, oh our brethren, the whole house of Israel,
Who mourn in this mourning,
We turn our hearts to our Father in Heaven,
The King of Israel and its Redeemer,
And we pray
For ourselves
And for Him:
Yitgadal, ve-yitkadash, shemah raba
Be-alema di vara khiruteh ve-yamlikh malkhuteh,
Ve-yazmaḥ ve-karev meshiḥei...
That we may be worthy to live and see
With our very eyes,
Oseh shalom bimromav,
That He, who, in His mercies, makes peace in the heavens
Will make peace for us
And for all Israel.
And let us say:
Amen.

– Translated by Samuel H. Dresner

About the Author

S.Y. Agnon (1888-1970) was the central figure of modern Hebrew literature, and the 1966 Nobel Prize laureate for his body of writing. Born in the Galician town of Buczacz (in today's western Ukraine), as Shmuel Yosef Czaczkes, he arrived in 1908 in Jaffa, Ottoman Palestine, where he adopted the penname Agnon and began a meteoric rise as a young writer. Between the years 1912 and 1924 he spent an extended sojourn in Germany, where he married and had two children, and came under the patronage of Shlomo Zalman Schocken and his publishing house, allowing Agnon to dedicate himself completely to his craft. After a house fire in 1924 destroyed his library and the manuscripts of unpublished writings, he returned to Jerusalem where he lived for the remainder of his life. His works deal with the conflict between traditional Jewish life and language and the modern world, and constitute a distillation of millennia of Jewish writing – from the Bible through the Rabbinic codes to Hasidic storytelling – recast into the mold of modern literature.

About the Editor and Translators

Paul Pinchas Bashan (co-translator, "Young and Old Together") was born to Holocaust survivors in a D.P. Camp in Vienna, and grew up in Israel. Upon completing his military service in the IDF he moved to the United States where he initially worked for the Israeli Ministry of Defense in New York, working for several years in logistics and procurement, and finally becoming an executive recruiter. He went on to establish several successful executive search companies.

Sara Daniel (translator, "Introduction to the Chapters of the Book of State," "The Orange Peel," and "On Taxes") was born in Leeds and raised in London and Jerusalem. She studied literature in Ben Gurion University and Hebrew University, and is currently pursuing further studies in Bar Ilan University's Bible Department. A translator from her service in Military Intelligence, her recent translations include Binyamin Lau's *Jeremiah* and *Isaiah* (Maggid Books).

Samuel H. Dresner (translator, "Introduction to the Kaddish"), a rabbi, teacher, and author, served as rabbi of Moriah Congregation, Deerfield, IL, and later as a professor at the Jewish Theological Seminary. An author of significant works in the areas of Hasidism and Jewish life in America, he died in 2000.

Isaac Franck (translator, "The Kidnappers") was the executive vice president of the Jewish Community Council of Greater Washington, D.C., for twenty-five years. Born in Russia, Franck arrived in the United States in 1923, and received a doctorate in sociology and philosophy from the University of Maryland. Dr. Franck passed away in 1985.

Jules Harlow (translator, "Peace Everlasting"), ordained by the Jewish Theological Seminary, served as Director of Publications for the Rabbinical Assembly for more than thirty years, where he was responsible for editing and translating the *Mahzor for Rosh Hashanah and Yom Kippur*, the *Siddur Sim Shalom*, and other liturgical publications. His translations of Agnon's stories benefitted from having spent time with the author in Jerusalem, and serving as his translator during Agnon's tour of New York after receiving the Nobel Prize.

Rhonna Weber Rogol (co-translator, "Young and Old Together," translator, Y.L. Gordon, "With Our Young and Our Old We Shall Go") studied Hebrew from childhood at Shaare Zion Academy and Herzliah High School and later at Brandeis University and Hebrew University of Jerusalem. An attorney by profession, Rogol engages in volunteer work and Jewish and Holocaust education.

Jeffrey Saks is the Series Editor of The S.Y. Agnon Library at The Toby Press, and lectures regularly at the Agnon House in Jerusalem. He is the founding director of ATID – The Academy for Torah Initiatives and Directions in Jewish Education and its WebYeshiva.org program.

The fonts used in this book are from the Garamond family.

The Toby Press publishes fine writing
on subjects of Israel and Jewish interest.
For more information, visit www.tobypress.com.